KILLER WITCH IN WESTERHAM

Paranormal Investigation Bureau Book 6

DIONNE LISTER

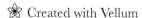

For my patient son, Evan. Love you. Love you lots xx

CHAPTER 1

I f happiness was chocolate soufflé, then this was sadness. I stared into my barren soufflé dish. All gone. Finished. Kaput. Finito. Fini. I sighed. The only way I was going to get more was to order another one—and look like a total pig—or lick the scant chocolate remains and probably get kicked out of The Ritz restaurant.

Will chuckled, his delectable dimples flashing at me from across the table. He looked oh so fine in his Persian-blue suit with white shirt and grey tie. The Ritz knew what it was doing when it implemented a dress code. "Before meeting you, I didn't know dessert could break a girl's heart."

"Well, now you know." I put on my most serious expression. "There's a name for it. Dessertdesertedaphobia."

"Sounds serious."

"It is. The only cure is more dessert." I nodded sagely.

"Well, then, I have the means to cure what ails you. I'll just order you another one."

I smiled. "You're the best boyfriend ever, but it's okay. My eyes are bigger than my stomach. I'll probably make myself sick. But if we're still here in thirty minutes, feel free to ask again."

He grinned, his blue eyes shining with happiness. "Consider it done."

How had I managed to end up with such a handsome, kind, thoughtful, and capable man? I quietly thanked the universe.

Now that dinner was finished, it was time to do what we'd really come here for. My smile dropped, and I pulled out my phone. "It's time, I think."

His smile faded. "You don't want to bask in the dessert afterglow a little longer?"

I shook my head. "Not even chocolate soufflé can make this easier." Words I never thought I'd say because, well, chocolate had done a pretty good job of comforting me thus far in life. I leaned forward and whispered, "I'm going to cast my no-notice spell."

He reached over, grabbed my hand, and stared into my eyes. "Good luck. Maybe we'll go for a walk in Green Park when this is done, check out the squirrels." He knew me so well. Squirrels were guaranteed to cheer me up. Cute, fluffy-tailed things, zipping about like they were on fast forward.

I smiled. "Thank you." I took in a trickle of magic and mumbled my spell. I grabbed my phone out of my red clutch. We were seated next to the windows, which were as tall as doors and framed by heavy drapery. The grandiose room screamed wealth, its soaring ceilings replete with a fresco of a cloudy sky, bronze chandeliers, and wall sconces, and statues set into arched wall niches. It had more than a touch of the French chateaus about it.

I could take a few photos from our table, but I'd have to get up and walk around because anyone seated on the far side would look small, not to mention, if my parents had their backs to where I sat, I wouldn't know it was them.

Taking a deep breath, I tamped down the unsettling stew of fear and anticipation that threatened to free my chocolate soufflé in the most unpleasant of ways. I craved these moments of trying to photograph my parents in a freeze-frame of history. But my talent was a curse. The soaring joy of seeing them was fleeting and always followed by the asphyxiating anguish of knowing they weren't actually there. My fingers could reach out for eternity and only ever find the whisper of a zephyr. My grief was more solid than they were.

But my talent was crucial in putting together the puzzle of what had happened to them and would likely lead us to Regula Pythonissam. They were the group of witches who were after me and had indirectly been involved in recent crimes in Westerham. Their endgame was a mystery we intended to solve before anyone else was killed, but I doubted it would be that easy. It felt as if we were playing catch-up.

I stood, put my arm in the air, and waved it above my

head. Not one head turned my way, but Will had an eyebrow raised. "What are you doing?"

"Making sure my no-notice spell is working. I always feel skittish when I use it. It's hard to believe no one will notice me doing something suspicious." I held my phone up, switched on the camera app, and said, "Show me my parents here ten years ago at lunch." I panned the phone to capture from one end of the room to the other.

A few tables that were full in real time showed as empty, and some that were empty suddenly had people sitting at them. I couldn't see my parents at any of the tables immediately surrounding us, so I carefully stepped away from our table and picked my way through the restaurant, viewing each table through my phone as I went. I sidestepped a waiter, narrowly avoiding total disaster. Yikes. I needed to be more careful.

A woman's laugh machine-gunned from a table to my left. She sounded like a drunk goat—well, what I imagined a drunk goat would sound like. I turned quickly and looked at her table but through my phone, and whoever had sat there the day my parents were here had been just as vulgar, but in a different way. A thirty-something-year-old man with dark, slick-backed hair that looked way too oily for anyone's good, was mid-conversation with two other businessmen. The guy's mouth was open, and his half-masticated food was on display. I gagged and turned away. Thanks, universe. Awesome freeze-framed moment… not!

I swallowed and refocussed. Now was not the time for being distracted. I wove between two more tables and stopped dead. My breath hitched, and my heart raced. There they were, sitting with three other people—a gorgeous, petite brunette woman who was maybe Japanese, and a man and a teenage girl whose backs were to me.

My mother's brow was furrowed as she stared across the table at the man whose face I couldn't see, likely listening to something he said. My father's lips were pursed, his expression screaming disapproval. But why? The Japanese woman's eyes radiated sadness as she looked at my mother. What was going on? I snapped various shots and moved around to the other side of the table so I could see who the man was.

I gasped, and my heart thudded, the whoosh of blood past my eardrums deafening. No. Freaking. Way. I squinted and blinked. But nope, I was really seeing what I was seeing.

Sitting next to an olive-skinned, Greek-looking man in his forties was none other than the younger version of Piranha.

My parents were having dinner with Agent Lam— before she was an agent—and... her parents?

Even though my thoughts raced and tumbled over each other in a futile attempt at making sense of the situation, I managed to snap a few shots. Teenage Lam wasn't a scowl-wearing narcissist. She had her hand on her father's arm, and her dark eyes held concern and worry. I knew this wasn't the full picture of who she'd been, but how did she get from this innocent-looking teen to the hateful psychopath we'd been dealing with?

And why were they having dinner with my parents? Had

Piranha known who my parents were all along? If so, there was no doubt she'd been after me the whole time. But why was I still alive or not kidnapped? She'd had plenty of chances.

I sighed and reached out towards my mother's shoulder, my breath hitching. I was only a couple of centimetres from her. The need to touch her vibrated up from my stomach, the pressure building, expanding to bursting. I couldn't hold it in any longer. Even though I knew heartbreak would be at the end of my fingertips, I settled my hand on her shoulder. Warm and firm. My eyes widened.

"Can I help you, miss?"

I started and wrenched my hand back, then lowered my phone. "Oh my God, I'm so sorry. I thought you were someone else." My cheeks heated. I blinked tears back. The older woman with white permed hair and a rounded face looked nothing like my mother. Crap. I was so stupid. What the hell had I been thinking?

Her smile was kind. "Not to worry." She turned back around, and her dining companion, another grandmotherly woman, gave me a gentle smile, then returned to her lunch. Well, my no-notice spell was blown—for these women at least. Plus, I'd gotten what I came for; actually, I'd gotten a lot more than I wanted. Time to return to my table.

Will stood when I approached. His tentative forehead wrinkles were mere snake trails in the sand as he assessed me. "I've paid the bill. Why don't we go for a walk?"

I nodded, not trusting myself to speak. He was so considerate, and he knew me better than I thought. Giving me a chance to possibly break down in a park where not many people would notice was a gift. Even with a no-notice spell, crying in a posh restaurant was not on my to-do list.

I donned my coat and grabbed my bag—Will's jacket was warm enough for him. A true Englishman, he didn't wear a coat until it was less than ten degrees Celsius. He took my hand and led me outside into the throng of pedestrians hurrying around under grey skies. A cool end-of-October breeze nudged sunset-coloured leaves off branches, sending them floating and twirling to the ground. One landed in front of me, and I stomped on it, grinning at the satisfying crunch. Will squeezed my hand, and we exchanged a smile. Even when I was sad, I tried to find happiness in the moment. And if the universe was feeling generous, I'd be able to string a few of those moments together.

Unfortunately, that was probably my quota for the day, considering I'd also just enjoyed delicious food and a romantic date with the man of my dreams.

We entered Green Park and meandered along the leaf-strewn path. Squirrels scampered between trees, and up and down trunks. So damn cute. "I want a squirrel."

Will laughed. "I don't think Angelica would appreciate having a squirrel messing up her house."

"But they're so adorable. It's as if they're on fast forward the whole time. I wonder how fast their hearts beat."

"Around two hundred and eighty beats per minute, depending on what they're doing. A hibernating squirrel only has a heart rate of around five beats per minute."

"Wow, how did you know that?"

"I once did an assignment on them in high school. As much as I'd love to educate you further about our furry little friends, I need to know what happened in there. You didn't exactly look happy when you came back. Did you see them?"

How would he react to news of Dana being there? Did he still have feelings for her? I mean, he'd said he didn't, but sometimes we lied to ourselves. And how would he react, seeing her young and innocent, gorgeous and kinder, more like the woman he'd fallen in love with?

"They were there, having a meal with another couple and their… daughter." I swallowed. Gah, why couldn't I be a squirrel? Having to do nothing but gather nuts sounded like a low-stress lifestyle.

"And?"

"The conversation seemed tense." I looked up at him. How to say what I needed to?

"What's wrong, Lily? Are you upset about seeing them?"

My nose tingled, and I swallowed the stupid lump in my throat. "I accidentally reached out to touch my mother, but I accosted an old lady."

He winced. "I'm sorry." He squeezed my hand again. "How did she react?"

I shrugged. "She was really nice about it. I didn't even get thrown out."

"That's always a good thing." He smiled but then let it fade. "I'm getting a sense that something else is wrong. Here, let me see the photos." He held out his hand.

"Um, before you do that, why don't we go somewhere private?"

He gave me a quizzical look and shrugged. "Okay. If you insist. Come on then." He turned, and we headed back the way we'd come. At least the toilets were at our end of the park. Will mumbled something, and the familiar tingle of his magic stirred the hairs on the back of my neck. Hmm, now that I thought about it, his magic did have a certain feel about it—it was warm and comforting with a hint of excitement and a sizzling undercurrent of power. Could other witches tell the difference in magic?

"No-notice spell?" I asked.

"Yes. Just in case anyone sees us go into the toilets and wonders why we don't come out again. There's a couple of people eating lunch out here, so they probably won't be going anywhere for a little while."

"Fair enough."

We reached the toilet block, and Will dropped my hand. "See you at Angelica's?"

"Sounds good. See you soon." We gave each other a quick peck on the lips and entered the small building. There wasn't an out-of-order cubicle because the facilities were too small, but it didn't matter. I went into the stall but didn't lock it. I counted slowly to twenty, to give Will time to get to the reception room and out of my way. I didn't think anything bad would happen if two people arrived simulta-neously, but it might mean we crashed into each other, and I didn't want to add physical pain to Will's day—what I was about to show him would be painful enough.

When I arrived, Will was holding the reception-room door open. "Took you long enough. Did you have to wait for the stall, or were you chickening out on showing me the photos?"

"No, and no. I was giving you enough time to get out of my way. Although you might wish I had chickened out after you see the pictures." I walked past him into the hallway and headed for the living room. He shut the door and followed.

Once we were seated next to each other on one of the Chesterfields, I took my phone out of my bag, and unlocked it. I brought up the photo app and clicked on one of the pictures showing Dana and her dad. "Here." His fingers brushed mine as he took the phone, but it wasn't the reason my heart raced. What if he still had feelings for her? What if one of them was love?

I studied his face so intently for clues that I probably looked like a desperate psycho. Lucky for me, or maybe not, it took practically no time for him to react. His eyes widened, and he sucked in a breath.

He stared at the screen. I stared at him. He made the image bigger and stared some more. His brow creased. I swallowed. I could really use the mind-reading talent right now. Was he just wondering what the hell Dana and her parents had to do with my parents' disappearance, or was he thinking teenage Dana was more gorgeous than he remembered, and he wished they hadn't broken up? Did he miss her even though she was an evil piranha?

Finally, he scrolled through the rest of the photos. When he was done, he went to my email app.

"What are you doing?"

His serious gaze met mine. "I'm messaging these to James and myself, but don't worry; I've spelled the email so that the photos can't be seen by anyone but James or me. If Dana or her group have somehow managed to bug our emails, they won't be able to see these."

I could see why James needed those photos, but I was pretty sure Will didn't *need* them. *Jealous much, Lily? Yep, guilty as charged.* Gah, I needed to get myself together. Will probably didn't want her back, but it wasn't as if he could just turn his feelings off. He was probably a bit shell-shocked at seeing her. I was such a bad friend. "Are you okay?"

A flash of emotion flickered in his eyes; then it was gone, replaced by the standard-issue PIB poker face. "Yes, I'm fine. You've done great work today, Lily. I have a feeling those photos will go a long way to helping us find out what happened to your parents. Are you sure you're okay after seeing them again?"

I shrugged and used my best "whatever" voice. "It is what it is. I'll be fine."

"Okay, good." He stood and handed me my phone. "While this is fresh in my mind, I'm going to duck into work and brainstorm, see if I can get a meeting with James. Is that all right?"

Um, no, definitely not all right. He obviously still cared for her way more than he would admit. I'd be stupid not to be worried. But there was nothing I could do. I gave him a weak smile. "Yeah, sure. Thanks for taking me to lunch."

"It was my pleasure. I'll see you later. Sorry for running off like this, but—"

"Yeah, yeah, I know. Work." I wasn't strong enough to hide the sadness in my eyes, so I let it all hang out. Pathetic was my middle name. "I hope you find what you're looking for."

"Me too, Lily. Me too." And without our usual goodbye kiss, he was gone.

CHAPTER 2

Eight thirty Sunday morning. I'd already been for my run and had a shower. Now I was settled at the kitchen table cradling a mug of coffee. A half-eaten double-chocolate muffin sat in front of me as I stared blankly at the wood grain in the table. Will and I hadn't had a chance to talk properly since the photo incident on Friday. At least he'd called last night and asked me out for dinner for tonight. I hoped we were going to be okay.

"You're up early for a Sunday, dear."

I jerked my head up, startled back into the real world. Angelica strode into the kitchen. Even though she wore casual clothes rather than her PIB uniform, she looked as immaculate as ever. She'd paired a black turtleneck jumper with dark blue jeans. My mouth dropped open.

"What's wrong?" She looked down at herself, maybe thinking something was out of place, God forbid.

"Um, nothing. I've just never seen you with your hair out on purpose. You look really good, almost like you've got a date or something." I chuckled. Angelica hardly went out, and she'd never had a date in the time I'd known her. Although, now that I thought about it, since she'd recovered from dying and being brought back to life during her undercover stint at the care home, she'd taken more time for herself and spent less time at work.

She smiled. "I'm off to London today to catch up with an old friend."

"Does this old friend have a name?" I waggled my eyebrows.

The corners of her lips twitched as she fought for control of the smile that would reveal too much. Too late. I grinned.

"His name is Edward. And despite what you think, this isn't a date. We're two old friends catching up." She recovered her stern face, gave me a warning glance, and sat opposite me. Her teacup appeared in front of her, already full of hot tea. "What's on your mind, Lily? You looked rather preoccupied when I came in."

Trust her to volley the conversation back to my side of the net. I should have known better than to let my guard down with her—casual clothes did not necessarily mean a harmless Angelica. "It's just... well. I know I'm being stupid, but Dana being in those photos.... I'm worried Will wishes he was still with her. It's not even his fault if he still loves her. Just because someone's horrible doesn't mean you automatically stop loving them."

Olivia sauntered in, ready for a lazy day if her tracksuit attire was anything to judge by. "Who's horrible? Did Will do something to you, Lily? If he did, I'll ask Beren to turn him into a fire hydrant, and then I'll gather the neighbourhood dogs and visit him." She wiggled her fingers and witch cackled.

I laughed "Good morning to you too."

"So? Spill." She sat next to Angelica, and a cup of tea appeared before her. "Thanks," she said.

"My pleasure, dear."

Their gazes locked on me expectantly. I sighed. I felt as if I was at an interview for a job I didn't even want. I waved my arm around and mumbled the bubble-of-silence spell. I didn't really need to wave my arm, but it let Olivia know I was casting a spell. Angelica would have felt the vibration of magic, but the small smile she wore indicated she probably enjoyed the drama of the silly arm wave.

Let's just rip the Band-Aid off. "The photos I took at The Ritz on Friday showed my parents having a meal with Dana and two people I assume are her parents. Will made sure to send the photos to his phone, and I've hardly spoken to him since." I hadn't had a chance to talk to Olivia since Friday because she'd stayed at her parents' on Friday night and been out with them on Saturday, then had gotten in late.

Her face froze as she likely decided what emotion to go with. Shock won. "Oh dear. I don't know what's worse: knowing they were all friends or Will wanting a picture of her on his phone."

Angelica shook her head while levelling a "what the hell

did you go and say that for?" look at my best friend before turning a calm look my way. "William is a sensible lad. Granted, he may still have feelings for her, but I'm sure they're closer to hate than love." She held her hand up. "And before you tell me love and hate are opposites sides of the same coin, they're not. I've known him for a long time, and while I can't tell you what's in his head right now, I do know he's absorbing the information and dealing with it in his own way. He knows this is difficult for you too, Lily, and he probably doesn't want to make it worse by telling you anything before he's had time to think it through. Just be patient. He normally takes a few days to get his head together. Try not to worry, dear. Now, no more talk of those photos. We'll meet to discuss everything tomorrow night at seven. I've told everyone to be at your brother's."

Easy for her to say. "Okay. I'll be there. And as for being patient, I will, but it doesn't mean I won't worry. At least I've got a job this afternoon to keep me distracted."

Olivia leaned forward and her eyes lit up. "That's right. You've got the birthday-cum-reunion party. That should be interesting. I hear there's going to be a celebrity there."

"Oh, who?" I didn't really care about celebrities, but I didn't want to seem like a spoilsport—Olivia was so excited.

"I'm not sure. I've heard a couple of rumours at the station. Someone mentioned Emily Allcott, and someone else swore their mother saw Jeremy Frazer at Costa on Friday." She smiled. "I hope it's Jeremy. He's so hot. Can you get me a signature?" She grinned hopefully.

"Who the hell is Emily Allcott?"

Olivia looked at me as if I'd said I didn't know who the Queen was. "Only one of the biggest stars on English television right now. She's in the number one police procedural, *On the Streets.*"

"Never even heard of it. Sorry."

"It's okay, Lily. You can't help being an Aussie. And I shouldn't be surprised, really. I mean, you love Vegemite." She shuddered and pretended to gag.

"Ha ha, very funny. You're a comic genius." I rolled my eyes.

Angelica stood. "Have a lovely day, ladies. I'm off to London." She waved, then disappeared.

Olivia gawked at the spot Angelica had just vacated. "I don't think I'll ever get used to that."

"Yep, I know the feeling. I still get a shock when people appear in my camera right in front of me when they're not really there." She gave me a sympathetic look. No doubt, she was thinking about my parents. I shrugged. "So, what are you doing today?"

"Just hanging out here. It's the first day off I've had for ten days. I'm going to catch up on some TV. It's a binge-watching kind of day." She grinned.

I smiled. "Sounds good." I finished my breakfast, magicked everything away, and stood. "Well, have fun. I'm going to get my stuff packed up. The family reunion birthday thing is at this lady's house. She wants me there early to get some photos of them setting up. Weird, but whatever. It's going to be a long day. I'm there until late tonight." I probably shouldn't complain because the money was good, but being on my feet all day directing people would be draining. Hopefully, they'd be happy with me getting lots of candid shots too. I enjoyed those because I could be more creative, and I didn't have to talk to anyone.

"Maybe we could get some home delivery tonight. Indian?"

"Definitely. I'll text you when I'm on my way home. Make sure you order the vindaloo." Mmm, spicy food was the best.

She grinned. "Will do. See you later."

I waved as I walked out the door. Time to get to work.

CHAPTER 3

My client Marcia Ferndale lived in Crockham Hill, Edenbridge, which was about a mile and a half southwest of Westerham. My assimilation to UK life was almost complete now that I was thinking in miles instead of kilometres. I wasn't sure if that was a good thing or not. Melancholy filled my lungs, and I sucked in more air as I tried to dispel that suffocating sensation. Sorrow was a terrible substitute for oxygen.

I tried to shake off the need to return to Sydney as I turned into Mrs Ferndale's driveway. Angelica had kindly lent me her car. I'd considered buying one, but I hardly ever needed it, and neither did Angelica, so we decided I should just share hers.

Near-naked trees lined either side of the long drive, their orange and brown leaves an autumnal carpet marking the way to the house. I soon emerged into a bitumen-paved open area almost filled with cars. They started parties early around here. Luckily, there were still a couple of spots left, so I took one.

Before I got out, I took a moment to focus and just breathe. While I did that, I checked out the elegant two-storey reddish-brown-brick home that faced the parking area. Its multi-paned, white-framed windows made it look like a doll's house. There were lots of trees around, but very little grass, and no garden. Not exactly inviting, and definitely not a place to take family photos, unless dreary was what they were going for.

Tap, tap, tap. I jumped and gasped, narrowly avoiding a heart attack. I turned my head to the right, my heart hammering. A guy stood there smiling. *What the ever loving?* I opened my door.

"Oh, sorry. Did I scare you?" His familiar blue eyes sparkled, and his smile turned into a smirk. Yeah, he was real sorry. And too damn attractive. He was probably used to women falling all over themselves to get his attention.

I gave him my sarcastic smile, which was my first line of defence—it usually worked. "No, you didn't scare me. I jump around randomly every now and then. It's a bad habit, but it helps me stay fit." And then it hit me. That's where I'd seen him before. Olivia was right—there was a superstar at this get-together. Jeremy Frazer. He was the romantic-comedy man of the moment. His sandy-blond hair and tanned skin added to his appeal, although whether his tan was natural or fake was anyone's guess. I hated to admit it, but he was even better looking in real life. Not that

I was interested. Olivia was going to kill me, but there was no way I was going to ask for his autograph—it would stoke his ego, and that flame was big enough already. Fame, to me, was a turnoff rather than a turn-on. Maybe I was being unfair for assuming he'd be self-absorbed, but I was willing to take that risk.

I got out of the car, but he didn't move back, which left mere inches between us. Awkward much?

"So, which one of my lucky cousins are you dating?"

I shut my door and went to the boot. "None. I'm the photographer." I would have liked to have said something snarky, but he might have been Mrs Ferndale's favourite grandson, and I didn't want to upset the client. As I lugged my equipment bag, tripod, and reflector out of the boot, he walked around to join me.

"Here, let me help."

Well, that was unexpected. I handed him the tripod. "Thanks."

"This hardly weighs anything. Why don't you give me that bag? It looks heavy."

I appreciated his offer, but I didn't trust him not to drop my thousands-of-dollars-worth of equipment. "Thanks, but I'm good. Can you just close the boot?"

He shut it. "Done. Now let me show you to the house." He smiled, again revealing straight, white teeth—a true movie-star smile. Unfortunately, he stayed that way for a beat too long. Was he waiting for something? Oh, yeah, probably for me to recognise him. Not going to happen.

"Ah, thanks." I smiled awkwardly, or was I grimacing?

Were we going to stand here all day? I turned and made my way to the house—Mrs Ferndale was expecting me two minutes ago.

"Wait up." Awkward famous guy caught up to me. "Are you usually this unfriendly?"

"I'm not being unfriendly. I was supposed to be here at a certain time, and I hate being late for a job. Unfortunately, Mrs Ferndale isn't paying me to stand around and chat."

"Fair enough, but would it hurt you to smile?"

I stopped dead and stared at him. He halted and turned. Oh, the things I wanted to say. "Look, I'm not here to—"

"Hello! You must be Lily." A little old lady—clichéd but true in this case—in cream slacks and a floral-print blue shirt stood at the front door waving her frail slim arm and smiling. It was probably lucky she'd interrupted me, or I might have lost this job before I'd started.

I speed-glared at Jeremy and hurried to the front porch. "Lovely to meet you, Mrs Ferndale." I smiled.

"Welcome, Lily. And please call me Marcia."

"Thanks, Marcia."

"Now, why don't you come in, and I'll show you around. Then you can get started. Almost everyone's here already. So many of my family have come from all around the UK, and I love them staying here." It was a big house, but from the number of cars out front, it would have to be like the Tardis to fit everyone. She must have seen my sceptical expression. I still had poker-face work to do. "The house has six bedrooms, but I also have a three-bedroom barn conversion out the back. We're on two acres."

"Nice. I can't wait to have a look."

"Well, then, let's go." She turned and went into the house. I followed, the annoying movie guy behind me. I hoped he was going to leave me alone now he knew I was an unsmiling cactus.

No such luck.

"So, Lily," he said. "What brings you to England?"

"My brother moved here and suggested I come over. I figured, why not?" He didn't need to know that I was really a witch, my brother was kidnapped, and the PIB basically dragged me over here. I smiled to myself. My life sounded like it could be a movie—not a romantic comedy though, more like a confusion of comedy and drama with a bit of thriller thrown in for good measure.

As we walked from the entry foyer past the formal lounge and through to the large family room at the back of the house, I drew a small amount of magic and checked out Marcia's aura. She was a witch. I turned and checked Jeremy out. He winked. Oh brother. I turned back quickly and resisted an eye-roll. But yep, he was a witch too. Wow, there were more around than I thought, not that I checked people's auras often—I never remembered. It was likely her whole family were witches. I didn't need to know, so I didn't bother checking anyone else.

This room had polished parquetry flooring and a huge, modern, open-plan kitchen to the right, and through a set of double doors at the back was what looked like a glass-roofed conservatory. All in all, it was a nice space... filled with Marcia's family. A ten-seat timber dining setting to the left was fully occupied by six adults and four kids. They gave a combination of smiles and waves when I looked their way.

"Hi." I smiled.

Marcia introduced everyone by name and who they were to her: two of her daughters, one son-in-law, one balding son, his two daughters who must have been around twenty, and four grandkids who ranged in age from four to ten. They were her eldest son's, eldest son's children. Confused: who me? I just smiled and nodded—there was no way I was going to remember everyone's names. Maybe I should have suggested they wear name tags.

She led me the opposite way, to the kitchen area, where her eldest son, his wife, and Jeremy's brother were chatting and cleaning up after breakfast.

"So, that's everyone who's in the house right now. My brother, his adult children, and grandkids are out walking, and I have a few cousins who are arriving in an hour." She clasped her hands together, her smile broadening.

I couldn't help but grin at her enthusiasm. She was obviously excited to be celebrating her birthday with her whole family. I wished I already had my camera out—it would have made for a great shot. "Can I have a look around the garden? Is there anywhere specific you'd like some of the shots taken?" I crossed my fingers that the backyard was prettier than the front.

The doorbell rang. Marcia clapped her hands together. "That must be Ross and the girls. I'll be back. Jeremy, do you mind showing Lily the garden?"

"Sure thing, Gran." He turned to me as she hurried

away. She sure moved well for an eighty-year-old.

One of the middle-aged women at the dining table stood and strode over. She was as tall as Jeremy, around five foot eleven, and had the same blue eyes and straight nose. She put her arm around Jeremy. The hand that dangled over his shoulder had bright-red manicured talons dripping off it. Add in the chunky gold diamond rings, and it was as glittery as a ridiculously expensive Christmas tree. All but ignoring me, she said, "Sweetie, if you're too tired, I can show the photographer around. You shouldn't be bothering with such mundane stuff."

Jeremy scowled and shrugged her arm off. "I'm fine, Mum. I want to show Lily around, actually."

His mother turned her gaze to me but didn't smile. She didn't look angry, exactly, more as if she was assessing me and found me lacking. Maybe she was being protective. She probably knew women would be after him for more than his good looks. Celebrities attracted users. Fame was a double-edged sword. Jeremy shook his head and stood between his mother and me. "Come on, Lily. Let's go. Gran wants to get started on those photos." He led the way to the conservatory and to the yard.

A small area of brick paving connected the rear of the house with the yard, which was a fairly level lawn that ran about fifteen metres and ended in a hedge with a door-sized gap in the middle. Intriguing. "Where does that go?"

He smiled—this time it was genuine, not creepy. "Why don't I show you?"

I smiled and nodded. As we stepped into the green

corridor, he asked, "Left or right?"

"Oh, wow. Is this a hedge maze?"

His smile widened to a grin. "It sure is. I spent many happy hours exploring it as a kid. Of course, I knew it back to front, but sometimes, I'd take a book, sit in one of the 'rooms,' and read. So, left or right?"

"Right."

The hedges were close together, so we could only walk single file. There would be just enough room to squeeze past another person if you had to, but you'd get jammed into the hedge. Jeremy let me go first. The air was still and frigid, the ground soft from recent rain. The hedge was at least two foot taller than me, and only a haze of sunlight filtered into it, creating a surreal, otherworldly atmosphere.

We turned a sharp left and in a few metres came to a T-intersection, at which I chose to turn left. After three more turns, we came to an enclosed area that was just big enough for the park bench and pedestal-style bird bath in its confines. "One of my reading spots. It was great for escaping my mother—she doesn't like the maze." His smile had disappeared, and he worried his bottom lip between his teeth. "Um, sorry about before. Even though she can drive me crazy, she, my brother, and I are close. We stuck together after my father left when I was ten. Mum's super protective of me. She's paranoid that women want to use me." He shook his head. "And is that such a bad thing anyway?" His half-hearted grin was lopsided, and I could see why he was the current darling of the cinema.

"I don't know. Is it?" Okay, so I thought it was, but this

was me being diplomatic.

"I asked you first."

I shrugged. If he wanted honesty, that's what he'd get. "It depends on whether you're using them too. If not, I can see how it would get tiring and depressing to have people hanging around hoping a bit of fame rubs off on them. And I guess you'd never know if they were there because they liked you for you, or if it was just the fame."

"Gotcha!" He shot me once with his finger pistol.

I wrinkled my brow. *What the hell?*

"You *do* know who I am."

"Yeah, yeah, I recognised you, but fame doesn't impress me. Sorry. I like to go by who the person is. Are they nice? Yes—awesome. No—they can take a hike."

He nodded, his expression thoughtful. "I can respect that."

"Great. Is there—"

"Jeremy! Jeremy, I need you inside now!" came from outside the maze.

He rolled his eyes.

"Jeremy!"

"I have to go. Are you finished here?"

"Is there any more to the garden other than the maze?"

He nodded. "When you come out of the maze, turn right and walk around it. At the back is an informal garden, weeping willows, and a stream. There's also a tall hedge to the right, and the barn conversion's on the other side of it, but I don't think you need to see that. Up to you. I'll see you inside soon."

"Thanks."

I followed him out of the maze, to his scowling mother. She stabbed me with her gaze before turning to her son and softening her expression. "Gran needs help with the sandwiches." While he'd been irritating when we'd first met, he hadn't been so bad since then, and right now, he had my sympathy. He'd actually turned out okay for someone with such a strange parent.

I wandered around the border of the maze further into the yard, my shoulder aching from the weight of my equipment. I opened the bag and took out my Nikon. My button-pushing finger itched to get started.

At the end of the maze, the land sloped gently down to a line of weeping willows. That must be where the creek was. In between the maze and willows was an expanse of grass interspersed with mature trees. Drooping white-petalled blooms and happy yellow bulbs flowered amongst the fiery leaf litter in the dappled shade of the shedding trees. Birds hopped from branch to branch and flitted from tree to tree. I squeed at a group of squirrels who scrambled up and down the trunk, manically changing their minds about whether they wanted to be on the ground or in the tree.

I framed the scene and took a few snaps. I'd definitely get Marcia and her clan out here later for a group shot. I checked my watch—I'd been here for twenty minutes. Gah, time to get a move on. I hurried down to the line of melancholy trees bowing over the creek. It was a fair distance away, and I was puffed when I reached them.

The stream was pretty much a river, spanning at least

four metres bank to bank. The water flowed lazily, but the bent rushes on both banks indicated fast-flowing water had recently trampled through. The air was cooler amongst the willows. Matching trees framed the opposite side, a forest of autumnal brilliance at their backs. So pretty.

I brought my camera to my face and focussed the lens. There was more shadow than light, and to get the best pics, I'd need my tripod so I could slow my shutter speed without compromising on clarity. I clicked off a couple of test shots. Although the light would change before I was out here again, it would still be good to have a reference. I focussed on the wood's golden hues, and the light dimmed, the only illumination coming from the full moon shining above. What the hell? I hadn't blocked my magic—I hated to do it, and normally I only did it to avoid copping a see-through person in my viewfinder.

Across the water, a body appeared on the ground between the willows and thicker woods. My heart raced. Dead bodies had never appeared unasked before. Was this going to be my new normal? I blinked away the tears burning my eyes.

Crap.

The woman's long hair fanned out around her head, and she was dressed in some kind of long formal dress, which hugged her body, but I couldn't tell the colour in the dark, which was a good thing, considering. The skin on her face was gone, and a heart-shaped hole had been cut out of her dress on the left side of her chest. Had someone cut out her heart? My head spun as blood drained from my face. *Get it together, Lily. You can't tell, so stop guessing and freaking yourself out.* It was too dark to discern if there was a wound. I swallowed my horror as I clicked the shutter button several times. I wasn't sure if the image would wait for me to change to a zoom lens, but I had to try since I couldn't cross the water—it was too wide and deep, and there was no bridge—yet I couldn't get much detail. I swapped lenses and tried again.

Nope. Damn it! She was gone. I took a few deep breaths and stared at the spot across the river without my camera filtering the view. That poor woman.

My phone rang, and I jumped. I fished it out of my pocket with shaking fingers. "Hello?"

"Lily, where are you? Everyone's arrived, and we're waiting for you in the conservatory. It's time to start the photos."

"Ah, I'm just checking out your gorgeous property. I'll, ah, be there in two minutes."

"Goodo. See you soon."

I lifted my camera one more time, but no luck. I didn't want to call on my magic, in case someone inside felt it and wondered what I was doing. What if Marcia or one of her family had murdered this girl? Or what if she was one of them, and they didn't want to be reminded? Not to forget that I couldn't explain how I knew about the body. I'd have to text James and tell him to research it quietly.

I grabbed my phone and photographed two of the photos showing on my Nikon's screen. Then I typed out a text, added those photos, and pressed Send. As I was walking back to the house, the phone rang. I didn't even need to look at the screen. "Hey, James. I'm just at a job. I can only talk for about thirty seconds."

"Jesus, Lily. Are you okay?"

"Yeah, I'm fine. A bit shaken, but I couldn't get very close, and it was dark, so I didn't see every gory detail. I have no idea how long ago it happened, but it was at night. Not sure what season either."

"Okay. I'm going to get Millicent to run a check on missing persons. This could've happened twenty years ago, for all we know."

"Yeah, I suppose so. Although I have a feeling it wasn't quite that long ago. Her hairstyle and dress didn't look that old-fashioned, but then again, it was dark." The conservatory door was open, and Marcia was waving. "I gotta go. I'll call you when I get home tonight."

Today was going to be a long day while I waited to find out about the mystery woman. Who killed her and why? Who was she? She'd looked as if she was in her late teens— way too young to die.

I pushed my shoulders back and pasted on a smile. Then I walked through the door... into complete mayhem.

A man I hadn't yet been introduced to stood with hands on hips, toe to toe with Jeremy's mother. He was shouting. "Damn it! How many times have we been through this?" Three of the younger children were running around the family room. One of them had some kind of food—which may or may not have been bacon—and was dangling it in front of a small, brown terrier, who was doing its best to grab it. It barked as it chased the laughing, squealing kids. One of Marcia's older granddaughters was yelling at the kids to stop. Jeremy was nowhere to be found.

"Lily, I'm afraid things have gone rather pear-shaped." Marcia placed a gentle hand on my arm.

"Hmm, yes. Would you like me to get some shots, or is this something you'd rather forget?" I turned to her with a wry smile.

She stared at the fray, a thoughtful expression on her face. She shrugged and gave me a cheeky grin. "Why not? I'm only eighty once. Maybe one day we'll look back at this and laugh."

I grinned and changed lenses to my 50 mm. I focussed on Jeremy's mother, who was waggling her finger in front of the other man's face as she ranted. Gah, I hated when people did that. *Click*.

The dog growled. An earnest game of tug of war between the young girl and dog played out on the floor. I moved carefully—so as not to startle anyone—but swiftly towards them. *Click, click*. I'd snapped off quite a few pics when the dog wrenched its head sideways, securing the salty morsel once and for all. Game over. Dog: 1, little girl: 0. Although she was giggling. I was sure she felt like the winner for all the fun she'd had. I took a few pics of her enjoying the moment before I turned to eyeball what else was going on.

Ding dong, ding dong, ding dong, ding dong. "Oh, for heaven's sake! Hold your horses." Marcia hurried to answer the doorbell. I went with her, ready to take more photos—who knew,

I might get a great reunion picture of her greeting someone she hadn't seen for years.

I pointed my camera and focussed on the front door. Marcia opened it. I click clicked. Jeremy, cheeks flushed and face set into a stony expression, pushed past us and slammed the door on an army of photographers jostling and shouting behind him. I lowered my camera and bit my bottom lip. Marcia and I shared a worried glance before she went after him.

Not wanting to add to the unsettling start to the day, I cut off access to my magic. The void that opened inside me left me yearning for *something*. It was like an itch you couldn't scratch, one that was bone deep and all-consuming. *Suck it up, Lily.*

I lifted my Nikon to my face—hiding behind it. Even though I knew people could still see me, a sense of security and the possibility of getting candid shots that cut through the veneer my subjects presented to the world thrilled me. Even with the void, I was the proverbial pig in mud.

"Who told them I was here?" Jeremy faced his family, hands on hips. "I'm waiting." His family's concerned gazes pinged from him to each other.

Finally, his mother said, "Well, you won't stay famous if nobody hears about you for a week. Give the public what they want. I've sacrificed too much to see you waste it all because you want privacy." Sadness shadowed her eyes. "When you're gone, I miss you terribly. The sooner you can come home for good, the better." Okay, so maybe some of her anger was driven by fear of losing him. She really did care.

I'd slowly orbited the crowd, and I stood side-on so I could snap both Jeremy and his mother's faces. I wasn't sure if Marcia really wanted this recorded, but I wasn't going to interrupt and find out. She could always ask me to delete everything later.

Jeremy's face slackened. "You? *You* sacrificed? You used to complain when you had to drive me to auditions when I was a teenager. You begged me not to take jobs overseas, and when I did, you refused to talk to me until I came home. I'm the one getting up at five in the morning and working twenty-hour days for weeks on end."

"But you don't understand—" She reached out to him.

He put his hand up. "I don't want to hear it."

Jeremy's brother put a calming hand on his arm. "Why don't we go upstairs and cool down. What about a game of *Assassin's Creed?*" The brothers looked at each other, their eyes filled with meaning only those two understood.

The brothers turned and walked towards the stairs to the upper floor.

"Get back here, now!" His mother started after them.

"Let them go, Catherine." Marcia put herself between the fleeing young men and her daughter. "Don't ruin my birthday again, or you won't be invited next year."

Catherine took a step, and someone—I had no idea who —whispered, "Inheritance."

My eyes widened. Really? Who were these people?

Although, Marcia wore a smirk. Had she said that? I wasn't sure if I was more or less disturbed.

Jeremy and his brother had disappeared up the stairs, and my camera was trained on Marcia and her self-satisfied grin.

"Hey, camera girl. It's time for you to leave. I think you've seen quite enough." A burning tingle zapped along my arm. Was Catherine going to hurt me with magic? I snapped open my portal to the magic river and created a return-to-sender spell.

An invisible force shoved me as her spell met mine. I stumbled back but managed to keep my feet. Catherine wasn't so lucky. She flew backwards and landed on her bottom. I blinked. What had she tried to do to me?

The gaggle of family, young and old, stared, mouths agape.

Marcia was first to recover. "What in God's name did you do that for? If you weren't my daughter, I'd be calling the PIB right now." She turned to me. "Are you all right?"

My heart thudded a thousand beats per minute, but other than that, I was pretty sure I was okay. I looked down at myself just to make sure. Yep, no frog legs or missing anatomy. I checked my camera. It was okay, and the photos seemed to still be there.

"I think I'm okay. What spell did you cast, and why? I haven't done anything wrong."

She slowly stood, glaring at me the whole time as if it were my fault she'd fallen. Well, it was kind of my fault, but not really. If she had kept her witchiness to herself, none of it would have happened. "I don't trust you. You'll sell those photos to the media, make my son look bad."

"You mean make you look bad." Marcia rolled her eyes. "I truly am sorry, Lily."

"So she tried to delete my photos?"

She turned to Marcia. "I'm just protecting my son. Has everyone forgotten about that crazy stalker who almost killed him?" Marcia frowned and shook her head slowly. Catherine turned back to me.

The fact that Catherine was happy to ruin a human's morning of work annoyed the squirrel happiness out of me. Gah, what a mess.

Bong, bong, bong. The deep chimes silenced the chatter. "Never a dull moment around here," said the balding old guy—I'd forgotten his name, and honestly, there were too many for me to remember. "Do you want me to get it, love?"

"Yes, please," said Marcia. "But we're not expecting anyone else. If it's another grimoire salesman, I'll scream." Door-to-door grimoire salesmen were a thing? Who knew?

"Canape, anyone?" Huh? One of Marcia's adult granddaughters held out a plate of little savory pastries. They smelled delicious, but timing…. Adults and children hovered around the platter and dug in. It was always a good time to eat in this house, apparently. Maybe they were all used to the drama?

"Marcia, if you would rather I came back later this afternoon, when everything's settled down, I'd totally understand, and I'd be happy to deduct some of my fee." Why would she want all the bad stuff recorded? We had enough for the day. We really did—well, at least I had.

"Oh, no, Lily. I want everything documented." She gave me a reassuring smile.

"Ah, okay. If you're sure."

"Extremely, but only if you're okay to stay after that incident. And actually, I'm going to give you a bonus for having to put up with that." She shot a death glare at her daughter, then looked back at me. "I truly am sorry. If she tries anything else, I'll kick her out."

"You wouldn't!" Jeremy's mother's eyes were wide.

"Try me, Catherine." Marcia lifted her chin, her back ramrod straight. Was she really eighty today? She could easily pass for forty right now with all the "I'll take you on" vibes she radiated.

Catherine's tone regressed to a whingy five-year-old. "But I was only trying to protect our family. Why do I always get blamed for everything?"

Marcia shook her head.

"Just wait here, and I'll get Jeremy." The bald guy—I think it was Marcia's brother—returned with the witch who had arrived via the reception room. Not a grimoire salesperson, apparently. Just for fun, I took some shots of the new girl, who looked to be in her late twenties. She wore a sexy red dress and matching shiny red platform heels. Her straight blonde hair was in a pixie cut, and her artificially plumped lips were painted scarlet. She was gorgeous except for her huge lips, which were so obviously tampered with that they looked weird. Subtlety, people, subtlety.

Why did so many women embiggen their lips? It was such a thing, even with women my own age and younger. What was wrong with normal human lips? Since when did they become not enough? I had a huge suspicion we were all being conned by plastic surgeons. I mean, why were all the ones on television men who needed to take their own advice and have Botox and their lips plumped according to their definition of beauty, yet we were the ones forking out for something we didn't need? I should come up with a spell so that we all thought we were beautiful regardless of our lip plumposity.

Catherine bore down on the new girl. "Do you work with my son, then?"

"I did."

"So, what are you doing here?" Catherine folded her arms. I hoped the new girl had her return-to-sender spell up —she was going to need it.

"I heard he was coming back here for his grandmother's birthday, and since we're together, it's only right that I should be here."

Catherine looked her up and down. Her smile, when it materialised, was not kind. "You're not his type. He doesn't go for slutty Americans, and your accent is terrible. So common."

My mouth dropped open. I was about to defend the poor girl when Jeremy came down the stairs. His face drained of colour. I felt bad, but I pressed the camera button. *Click, click.*

The new woman's adoring smile lit up the room. Something didn't add up.

"Who let her in? Jesus. Get her out before I call the police." Jeremy lifted his hands, and the warmth of someone using magic prickled my scalp. I wasn't sure whether to be excited I was getting all this on camera or if I should be worried someone was about to get hurt.

"But I love you!" The woman—no one had bothered to introduce her, but if she knew she wasn't going to be welcome, no wonder she hadn't said anything—ran towards Jeremy.

Click, click, click. Ooh, action shots. She launched herself at him, arms wide. Jeremy mumbled something, and the air in front of him shimmered. The woman slammed into an invisible barrier. She screamed, and blood gushed out of her nose. On some level, I knew this was horrible, but I kept snapping away. Well, no one had told me to stop....

The woman ugly cried. Her red-smeared hands hung uselessly at her sides while her nose bled all over Marcia's floor. Jeremy's mother looked at him. "What's going on?"

"She's a stalker. I worked with her on a show ten years ago. Can someone please get her out of here?" The fear in his eyes was genuine.

"But you said you loved me! What about when we got married? You can't treat me like this. I'm your wife." Everyone was looking from Jeremy to the woman and back again. It was more drama-filled than a Wimbledon final or an episode of the *Kardashians*.

"What?!" his mother screamed. "You're married?"

His brow wrinkled as he scowled. "No. Of course not.

We got married in the TV show we were in. For God's sake, what's wrong with all of you? If you don't get her out of here in one minute, I'm leaving."

Marcia stepped up to the woman. "I'm sorry, but I'm going to have to insist you leave."

"But we're married," she wailed. She turned to Jeremy, her forlorn expression turning to anger. "Isn't it bad enough you tortured me by dating those hos. Haven't you put me through enough?"

Jeremy shook his head. His mouth set in a hard line, he turned and disappeared through a doorway. Hmm, where had he gone? Sympathy welled up for him. Yes, he was famous, rich, and gorgeous—what more could you want out of life—but he didn't deserve to be stalked by crazies. He was just a guy doing a job.

Catherine put her hands on her hips. "See? This is why I'm protective of my son. When will you people listen?"

Marcia glared at the stranger. "Leave now, or I'm calling the PIB."

My scalp prickled so much it itched. Catherine was mumbling something. Uh-oh.

The scorned woman glared at Catherine and growled before stepping through her doorway and disappearing—just in time, if you asked me. The itching stopped. I took a deep breath, relief freeing up my chest.

This wasn't the eightieth birthday I'd expected, and by the way Marcia rubbed her temples, it wasn't the one she'd expected either. Her gaze moved to me. "Lily, I give up. I think maybe you should come back tonight, for the dinner and cake cutting. I think we all need a break. See you here at seven?"

"Okay, Marcia. I'll see you back here then." I quickly scanned the room for my tripod, which was on the kitchen island. I gathered everything and went to the front door.

"Oh, and when you come back, feel free to use the reception room. Here are the coordinates." A piece of paper materialised in her hand, and she gave it to me.

"Thanks." I stepped out the door and into chaos. Crap.

How were these photographers allowed on private property? Why didn't Marcia call the police and have these people removed? Men shouted, "Who are you?" "Did you see Jeremy?" "What's going on in there?" "What's your name? Tell us your name, love." Shutters clicked over, and over, and over. I instinctively put my hand in front of my face, and adrenaline pumped through my body. Aggression crackled in the air as they shouted, stood in my way, and shoved cameras towards me. Someone shoved me, and I tripped sideways to collide with a snarling, balding guy with a diamond stud in one earlobe. Oh, the joy.

"Are you his new girlfriend? Is he getting married? Is that why you're here—to take the photos?" For God's sake. Bunch of morons.

"Come on, love. Give us a scoop."

I stopped. The pack halted. I looked around at them and took two steps forward. The idiotic sea of photographers did the same, and I almost laughed. It was like some comedy routine. Might as well have fun with it. I stepped two steps to the right, and my entourage followed. I stepped two steps forward, then two steps back. Oh my God! They did it too. I laughed. Totally absurd.

"I've got a scoop for you." The little voice in my head, the one that spoke sense and was rarely listened to, was saying something, but I couldn't hear over the naughty voice. I drew a tiny bit of magic and called into the void. I smirked. "You're standing in dog poo."

Everyone looked down. I'd managed to bring in enough dog poo to fit under four of the photographers' shoes. A few of them wrinkled their noses, and one said, "Oh, gawd. They're me best sneakers."

"Enjoy your day," I said as I pushed a space through them.

My shoulder aching from lugging my equipment around, I jogged to the car, dug my keys out of my pocket, and pushed the *beep-beep* button. The paps had started yelling questions at me again. Did they ever give up? How many scoops of poo did they want? I supposed I could find some more somewhere.

As I placed my bag in the boot, Marcia's angry voice came from the house. "Get out of here, you lot. I've just called the police. They'll be here shortly." Confirming her threat, sirens pealed in the distance. Finally.

I turned towards the driver's door and had to push one guy out of the way to get into the car. They moved quickly, these feral paps. They really were a smear on society. Just like poo. Once safely in the car, I locked the doors and started the engine. The sooner I got home, the better.

Funny how sometimes I could be so, so wrong.

CHAPTER 4

When I got home, I downloaded all the photos from the morning onto a hard drive, then wiped my camera card. I'd just started going through everything when my mobile pinged with a message from James. *Call me when you get home. It's urgent.*

Did he already have information on that woman I photographed? That was quick. I called him. "Hey, it's me."

"I thought you were working all day. Are you home already?"

"Yeah. Things got a bit crazy. I have to go back there tonight though."

"Okay. Hang on." There was mumbling in the background for a bit; then he came back on. "Can you meet with Angelica and me in her office in thirty minutes?"

"Yep. Is this about the photos I sent earlier?" Best to

confirm because what if it was about Will or Dana or the snake group?

"Yes, but don't talk about it with anyone. You haven't mentioned anything to the house owners, have you?"

"No, of course not. My talent is a secret. Remember?"

"Yeah, just making sure. Oh, and if there are any other photos, email them before you come. See you soon."

"Bye."

The first thing I did when I went back to my computer was send the remaining photos to James, as requested. I fought rising nausea as I attached the images to an email and pressed Send. Then, not wanting to dwell on the poor dead woman, I picked out a handful of nice pictures—the ones of the kids and dog before the day went pear-shaped—and started editing. I'd just do basic editing; then Marcia could pick the pictures she wanted, and I'd clean them up a bit more. As I worked, I had to wrestle my thoughts from the horror of the faceless woman a few times. My mind was like a petulant horse that didn't want to go where I tried to steer it. Stupid brain.

Who was she, and why had someone killed her? And even worse: Was the killer still out there doing his thing? And, yes, I'd assumed it was a man. How often did women do this sort of thing? Not often, if all the TV specials on serial killers were anything to go by.

I checked my phone. I was due at the PIB in five minutes. Time to leave. I made my doorway and stepped through into the sterile reception room. My old friend Gus answered when I buzzed. I chuckled to myself. What gross conversation was he going to make me suffer through today?

"Hey, Gus. How are you?"

"Great, Miss Lily. How are you?"

"Fine, thanks." Conversation starters to avoid: pets, food, work. What the hell was left? Traditionally, weather was universally considered a safe topic. Phew. "Quite a cool morning today, but at least it's not raining." I grinned, proud of myself.

"Yes, but that's what you get in autumn. I tell you what, though, the dog hates going outside to do his business, and after this morning, the misses threatened to get rid of him."

I was sure this demanded my horror and a follow-up question, but I didn't want to be dragged in that direction. I could see where it was going, and I wanted to cry. My voice was strangled when I replied, "Oh, no. That's not good." He couldn't make me ask, but I bet he didn't need the invitation to expand.

Sometimes, I hated when I was right.

He laughed. "No, not good at all. Lucky for me, he'd pooed as I was leaving for work, so I didn't have to clean it up. But it was on the carpet, and the smell." He waved his hand in front of his face. I wouldn't begrudge his wife if the dog was gone by the time Gus got home.

"Oh, look, here we are!" I turned to him and hoped my smile didn't look like a grimace. "Always great chatting. Have a wonderful day."

"Bye, Miss Lily." He opened Angelica's door and gestured for me to enter.

I walked through her unmanned reception area and into her office. "Hey."

"Hi, Lily. Thanks for joining us." Ma'am, as I usually thought of her at work, sat behind her huge desk, and James sat in front of it. I took the seat next to him.

"Hey, sis."

"This is *caj*. Why didn't we do this in the conference room?"

Ma'am leant back in her chair. "There's only three of us. We fit quite well here. There's no need to complicate things, dear."

"I'm okay with it." I smiled but then sobered. "I take it you discovered something about the woman I saw this morning?"

Ma'am nodded. "James can explain everything."

He turned in his chair to look at me. "The body you photographed was a young woman called Amanda Thomas. She was murdered ten years ago, her body discovered one morning in a forest five miles from where you took that photo. She grew up in Westerham, had an older sister, and was known to be a studious girl with a tight-knit group of friends. She was only eighteen." He fixed serious eyes on me. "The killer was never caught, and there have been two other similar murders since then, within a twenty-mile radius. The last one was seven years ago. No one's ever been arrested, and from the evidence, all the murders were done by the same person, but they left no DNA, no clues as to who they were. The only thing we have to go on is the personality profile done by an expert after the second body was found. We were never called in, so it's impossible to say whether there were traces of magic. If there were any, they'd be long gone now." A few sheets of paper, stapled together, appeared in James's hand. He gave me the bundle. "Give that a read, and let me know your thoughts."

What wasn't he saying? Both he and Ma'am watched me, faces unreadable except for the weight of assessment. So, what was I supposed to find? I started reading.

All murders happened within a three-year period. The women were between eighteen and twenty-two. As far as looks were concerned, there were two brunettes, and one blonde, all white skinned, two born in Westerham and one from "unknown." She'd had no ID and didn't match any reported missing persons.

I got to the crime-scene photos and gagged. They'd all had their faces and hearts removed. I shut my eyes and took a deep breath before continuing. Without a clear head, I wasn't going to be able to help. *Think, Lily, think.*

I opened my eyes and studied the police picture of Amanda. *Oh.* She was lying somewhere different in this picture from where I'd seen her. There weren't many trees. She was lying on grass, a stone church dominating the background. I furrowed my brow and looked up at James. "Whoever did this moved the body?"

"It looks that way. And there's no mention of dirt found on the body. Where you photographed her was full of leaf litter and mud. Surely that would have gotten into her hair, on her clothes, but the body was meticulously clean. We could sneak down there and take some samples, but any evidence would likely be long gone, unless there was jewellery or something. Or...." His gaze became tentative.

"Unless I go and ask the universe for more specific images?" My stomach dropped. My talent asked a lot of me sometimes. Looking at dead people and crime scenes was not my favourite way to spend the day. But these poor women needed justice, and what use was my talent if I couldn't help people?

"Before you answer, Lily, keep reading. You haven't reached the good part yet." Ma'am raised a brow and gave a nod.

"Ah, okay." The rest of the information was about boyfriends, friends, where they'd all been in the month leading up to the murders. My eyes widened. Oh, wow.

Two of the women had contact with Jeremy, movie star extraordinaire, although he hadn't been as famous back then. Considering where I'd seen that body, should I really be surprised? But was he a murderer? He was a little vain, but did that make him a killer? I shook my head. I didn't know him at all—having about thirty minutes of conversation hardly gave me insight into who he really was.

He'd briefly dated the woman I'd seen this morning. They'd recently broken up when her body was found. The police had interviewed him, considering links with the other two women. One of the others was a make-up artist who had done his make-up on a TV show he'd made a guest appearance in. Who the other one was, was anybody's guess. I sighed at the unfairness of it all.

The police had also questioned his mother. Yep, you'd

be mad not to with her anger-management issues. They'd discounted her as a suspect after that. Apparently she'd been the one to encourage their relationship—she had liked Amanda and was hoping she and her son would settle down together. She'd also had an alibi for the few days between Amanda going missing and her body being found—a sewing convention in Spain. Her alibi had been confirmed by other attendees. But being a witch, she could have travelled home and back without anyone noticing. Oh, it said she'd been sharing a room with another woman, and she confirmed Catherine had been with her pretty much the whole time.

So, there was a link with at least two of the bodies, but where was the motive, unless he was killing for the thrill of it? "Okay, so it's either Jeremy or someone who wants it to look like him. A disgruntled fan or adversary?"

Ma'am cleared her throat. "In between murders, Jeremy had ventured overseas, but he was always here when they occurred."

"He's a witch. Couldn't he just pop in and out whenever he wanted?" Dealing with witches was so much more complicated.

"True, dear."

"So, now what? I'm due back there tonight. I had to leave because this morning, another witch turned up claiming to love him. Apparently she's a stalker, and he told her to leave; then he disappeared to get away from her. After threats from Marcia—Jeremy's grandmother—she made a doorway and left. No one did anything violent, except when the woman tried to hug Jeremy, he made an invisible barrier, and she broke her nose on it. He didn't look like he was happy about it. I'm just not sure if he'd be the killing-for-fun type."

"But would he kill for peace and quiet?" James asked.

"If peace and quiet were that important to a person, why would they get into acting?" My brother was smart, but sometimes he said some really dumb things.

"Maybe he enjoys acting and got successful before he realised what it really meant."

I tilted my head down and raised my brow to look up at James with an "are you kidding me?" look. "Yeah, nah."

"Well, smarty-pants, can you get to know him a bit better tonight? Pay close attention to what he says, try and engage him in conversation."

Ma'am giggled. We both stared at her—she wasn't exactly known for giggling. She smirked. "Smarty-pants? Don't you mean smarty-boots?"

James and I exchanged a "what the hell" look and laughed. "Are you having us on?" he asked.

She shook her head. "That's what the more refined of us say. You Australians have no class." She soothed the sting of her words with a wink.

"You're just a bunch of weirdos. Smarty-boots...." I grinned and shook my head. "But to answer your question, James, yes, I can. I honestly don't get the killer vibe from him—he seems okay."

"Do you just think that because he's famous and attractive?" James raised his brows.

I considered it because I didn't want to be blinded by all

that—as much as fame didn't impress me, he *was* gorgeous. "Nope. Even if someone's good-looking, I would still pick up on roughly who they were. At least, I think so." Or maybe not. Was I fooling myself? How many people had been killed by people they trusted, people they never thought were capable of such a thing? And wasn't that how some serial killers managed to stay free for so long—no one saw it in them? Psychopaths were master manipulators.

"Just get what information you can, dear."

"Yes, Ma'am." Despite my initial feelings, I would be hypervigilant.

No psychopath was going to fool me. Nah ah. Now I just had to believe it.

CHAPTER 5

I returned to Marcia's home via my doorway. As much as I hated having my talent indicate someone was going to die soon, I again didn't switch it off. As horrible as it sounded, I didn't care if anyone here died, at least not in the grand scheme of things, and accidentally stumbling upon information could mean the difference between solving the murders and not. Besides, seeing Angelica and Beren as ghosts through my camera had been up there with the worst moments of my life, and no one in this house could top that. Perspective was a beautiful thing.

I knocked on Marica's reception-room door. Soon, it opened to reveal an extremely smoking-hot Jeremy in a black tuxedo and white shirt. Despite not wanting to give him any fuel to fan the fires of arrogance, I couldn't help swallowing. Even though I'd never cheat on anyone, let alone Will, I was only human.

Jeremy grinned, probably noticing my reaction. Gah. "Welcome to Gran's eightieth-birthday dinner. Come in." He stepped aside and swept his arm in a grand gesture of "come this way."

I smiled. "Thank you."

He closed the door and cleared his throat. "Ah, Lily."

I turned around. "Yes?"

His expression was earnest, apologetic. "I'm so sorry about this morning. The last person I expected to see here was my stalker. I also wanted to apologise for all the family drama you had to witness. I just hope you can...." He spread his arms out, palms upwards.

"Not tell anyone or show anyone the photos?"

He nodded. "Yes. Thanks for understanding. I figured you wouldn't say anything, and I didn't want to offend you by asking, but with my job, the smallest thing can derail a career."

I totally understood, and I wasn't a gossip. Except, could a murder investigation ruin a career? But, as everyone said, any attention was good attention, although I didn't subscribe to that theory. Hmm, the Kardashians were an exception. Who knew that if your sister made a sex tape, the whole family would be milking it for years, raking in the dosh? I'm sure people made a living out of worse things, but that still boggled my mind. How they were anybody's role models was beyond me. Our world was lacking something, and it clearly wasn't idiots.

"Any time. Plus, I would never break a client's confidence. What happens inside Marcia's home, stays inside Marcia's home."

"Thanks, Lily. You're amazing. I feel so much better now." He smiled. "Now, let's join the festivities. Gran's threatened my mother into her best behaviour, and I magicked a camera into the reception room after you left so we can see who's there. If they're not welcome, we won't answer it."

"Good plan."

He led the way towards soft background music and loud chatter. We walked through the family room, where a few people stood around talking, champagne glasses in hand, to the conservatory. I stopped at the door to the timber-framed glass structure and drew a quick breath. "Wow."

Two long tables sat side by side with enough space in the middle for someone to walk through. The crisp white tablecloths draped over them were weighed down by silver three-pronged candelabras and the white plates nestled between shiny silverware. The long-stemmed wine glasses at each setting reflected the pretty fairy lights strewn about the conservatory and the flickering candle flames.

Magical.

Marcia walked over to me. She was radiant in a shimmering black ankle-length gown, the three-quarter sleeves sleek on her slim arms. All dressed up, she didn't look a day over sixty-five. "Lovely to see you back here, Lily. Sorry again about this morning."

"That's okay. These things happen. Jeremy apologised too, but there's no need. It wasn't your fault, or his."

She smiled. "I appreciate you saying that. So, is it okay if you get started?"

"I would love to." My grin was genuine. Everyone was dressed elegantly, and the enchanting backdrop would make for some stunning shots. Plus, there wasn't an argument in sight. Jeremy was laughing about something with his brother while holding a two-year-old. His fair hair shone in the muted light, and when he turned, his gaze met mine, his blue eyes all but engulfed by dark irises. Way too sexy for my liking. I quickly turned away. I didn't want to give him the wrong idea. It was just that, well, how could he be a killer, and how could I not assess the likelihood of that while I was here? I felt sneaky, as if I was lying to everyone. There was no way I'd ever make a good spy.

I ducked back into the family room and set my bag and tripod on the floor in an out-of-the-way corner. I changed the settings on my camera for lower light and hung it around my neck before picking up the tripod. I turned and stood face-to-face with Jeremy. *Surprise!*

"Oops, sorry to scare you. I just wanted to see if you needed help carrying anything." Argh, how could I get angry at him when he was being so polite.

"Um, no. It's fine. I just wasn't expecting you to be there, and I've got this. I'm just going to set up my tripod over there to start with." I nodded towards fairyland, where one of the teenage girls was juggling three fireballs. What the hell?

Jeremy laughed. "Magic fireballs. They're not hot. Neat party trick, don't you think?"

"Ha! Very neat party trick, and good for giving people a heart attack. Crazy witches."

"Yep. We learnt from the best." He nodded towards his grandmother. "Anyway, let me know if you need anything… even a drink." He winked and went back to the party. He was so smooth. Since the display this morning when he met me at my car, he hadn't been sleazy or arrogant. Maybe he had a persona he used when meeting someone for the first time? Was his motto "do what they expect"?

I entered fairyland and placed my tripod between two chairs. I'd start by getting photos of the set-up. I was slowing my shutter speed slightly, so I'd need the added stability of the tripod to make sure my shots weren't blurry. I clicked my camera into the plate screwed onto the tripod and took my lens cap off. I spent a few minutes taking some gorgeous photos of sparkling silverware and opulence.

I raised the tripod and took some candid shots of Marcia and her guests. I knew some of the pics wouldn't come out well, as sometimes the subject was moving, which was never a good idea when you had a slower shutter speed. I'd get some clearer ones later when I could ask people to stay still.

In between snapping photos, I kept an eye on Jeremy as he socialised. Dinner came and went. Jeremy sat between his brother and Marcia, who was at the head of one table. They laughed throughout the meal and downed quite a bit of red wine, and who could blame them after the morning they'd had? I quietly moved around the table, taking photos as I went.

After doing the subtle thing, I asked diners to pose and smile. Once all that was done, I let Marcia know I was taking a toilet break before cake time. She silly-grinned at me, glassy-eyed. Her lovely English accent was crippled slightly by the effects of alcohol. "Thank you, sweet Lily. You don't know where the bathroom is, do you?"

"Actually, no."

"Well"—she looked around as if making sure no one was listening—"I'm not going to tell you." She laughed at her own joke before continuing. "My *handshome* grandson can show you." She waved her arm around above her head. Someone was going to have a hangover tomorrow.

I suppressed a giggle. "Ah, that's okay. If you tell me where it is, I'm happy to find it myself."

She waggled her finger in front of her face. "No, no, no. I've seen the way you've been watching him, and I know he likes you. I can tell." She gave an exaggerated wink.

My stupid cheeks heated—not because I liked him, but because everyone was going to think so. I was definitely not another groupie who crushed on famous men. Bloody James and Angelica. If it weren't for them asking me to observe Jeremy, I wouldn't be in this situation. And by the expression on Jeremy's face, he was of the opinion I was keen on him too. I suppressed an annoyed groan.

I gave Marcia an awkward grimace. "I've actually got a boyfriend." I was pretty sure it wasn't my imagination that Jeremy's face fell—he recovered with the speed of a squirrel running up a tree trunk, so maybe I'd been wrong. Who knew what my ego was capable of making me believe?

"Oh, that's a shhhhame." She frowned and stared at her empty wine glass, then picked it up and waved it around. She shouted, "Refill!"

I pressed my lips together to keep from laughing. Marcia was a funny drunk. I snapped a couple of shots of her enjoying herself before I lowered the camera and walked around the table to find the bathroom. Footsteps sounded behind me.

"Hey, Lily. I'll show you where it is, and don't worry about Gran. She's about as subtle as a sledgehammer."

I shrugged and smiled. I kept my voice light and as non-flirty as I could. "It's okay. I'm flattered she thinks I'm good enough for her grandson. Besides, I'm sure you don't need help finding someone."

"Ha, if only that were true." His smile resettled into a frown.

"How could it not be true? I say this without any intent, but you're attractive and successful, so surely you're beating them off with a stick. Jurors, I give you Exhibit A: this afternoon."

He sighed as we crossed the family room. Then he turned right, down a hallway. "But that's the problem. Because I'm famous, everyone thinks they know me. They don't know me. Like you said earlier today: I have no idea if people want me for me, or because they think I'm someone I'm not, or for the fame. You have no idea what it's like to disappoint people because you're not what they imagined. Most people I meet recognise me. They have a preconceived idea of who I am, and it's usually some fantasy they've built up in their own minds, their idea of the perfect man. And I'm not it. I'm not perfect, Lily." We stopped, and he gestured to a white door. "Here it is. Sorry for dumping that on you." He turned and strode back the way we'd come.

"It's okay," I called after him, but he didn't turn around. That hadn't gone well. What did he mean by he's not perfect? Did he mean *regular* not perfect, or *I'm a serial killer* not perfect? If I hadn't seen that body this morning, I wouldn't even be questioning what he meant. This whole thing was giving me a headache. And I felt sorry for him. Gah. He was rich, famous, good-looking, had family who cared about him, yet I pitied him. The world wasn't an authentic place for him. He was rarely seen for who he wanted to be seen as: himself. Seemed like a high price for him to pay. But it really was a first-world problem and one he should have seen coming. Still… he was just a person who needed to connect on a real level with other people.

As I sat on the loo, I figured out my next move. I had my phone in my back pocket. Did I dare sneak around the house and try and find evidence? If someone caught me, I could always say I was lost, but then how would I explain holding my phone out as if I was taking photos? Was it worth the risk? My heart thudded harder as I contemplated it. I wasn't one for confrontation, plus I didn't want Marcia to think ill of me. I rolled my eyes. I was such a scaredy-cat. *Think of the dead women, Lily. Fine! You win.* And it was totally normal for me to be arguing with myself. Surely everyone did it.

So, I would risk it, but I had to stay on the ground floor

—even *I* couldn't explain going upstairs away by saying I was lost. Or maybe I could pretend I really did have a crush on Jeremy, and I wanted to see where he slept. Gross. That was so bad. I couldn't live with people thinking I really would do that. Now my ego was getting in the way of gathering evidence. *Please don't talk yourself into going upstairs.* I waited for myself to answer. Phew, I had nothing to say.

I finished in the bathroom—yes, I definitely washed my hands with soap—and took my phone out as I walked into the hall. Still no text from Will. My heart constricted painfully. We'd hardly spoken since our lunch date and the bombshell I'd dropped on him about Dana. I tried to pretend his silence didn't matter, but it did. Even if he didn't want her anymore, he was going through something and shutting me out. Like I was a stranger.

Maybe I was. Maybe I didn't really know him at all.

I pushed the spreading pain into a ball and shoved it down deep where I could almost ignore it. Tonight was about my client and trying to find clues.

I listened, but there were no footsteps, just the soft distant sounds of the party. We'd passed one doorway on the way to the toilet, and further along, there was one more. I readied the photo app.

"Hey, you. What are you doing skulking about the hall?"

I jumped, flinging my phone into the air. I juggled it, batting it with one hand, then the other before I managed to curl my fingers around it. *Phew!*

Jeremy's mother strode towards me, hands on her hips, eyes narrowed.

"Just checking for messages from my boyfriend before I came back and took more photos. I hope that's okay." I hated being meek in front of bullies, but guilt needled me— I *had* been doing something underhanded. At least, from their point of view it was. I bet the dead women were on my side, though.

"My mother isn't paying you to slack off. Get back in there."

I blinked. Wow, she was rude. So damn rude. I hated that I couldn't tell her how horrible she was and storm out. How could the lovely Marcia have spawned this horrible woman? And in turn, how had this cranky bovine created Jeremy? Or was her contribution to him the serial-killer gene? Psychopaths were good at hiding who they really were, which meant Jeremy's mother was just a plain, mean cow. I sent a sorry to all the cows I had just insulted.

I bit my tongue and gave her my best death stare. I wouldn't say anything, but I wanted her to know I wasn't a pushover. As I walked past her, I held my head high. Maybe I should flirt with Jeremy, just to irritate her. But then that wouldn't be right—I had no intention of following through, plus I would hate it if Will was out there flirting with someone. Not cool. Why was revenge so damn difficult?

Maybe I could ask my magic to show me something when I took the legitimate photos. It was worth a try.

I grabbed my camera and got back to work. The cake had been set up on a small round table, which was also draped with stiff, white linen. The three-tiered work of art was like a wedding cake, consisting of round, white-iced layers. Red, pink, mauve, yellow, and blue icing flowers that looked almost real cascaded down the front of the cake and carpeted the base of the cake tray. Stunning. I took wide shots and close-ups.

I detached my camera from the tripod and wandered around, getting candid shots of people, but I also whispered my request to the river of magic. I should really ask James if I leached any power when I did this. How stupid of me that I hadn't already. I crossed my toes—my fingers were busy— as I whispered, "Show me the murdered girl from this morning." That was as good a place to start as any.

I angled my camera to look past everyone and into the family room.

And there she was.

She and Jeremy stood hand in hand chatting to Marcia by the kitchen bench, but it was an older kitchen to what was there now—70s style, if my assumption was correct. Orange benchtops and brown cupboard doors had been the height of fashion back then. What had they been thinking?

There was no way to tell what the date was, but it was daytime. I snapped a couple of shots, then turned around to face outside. The light wasn't bright. Cloudy, and maybe mid-afternoon? I snapped a shot of outside too—there might be a clue as to the time of year at least. The grass was greener than what it was at the moment, so maybe it was spring, maybe early autumn? There might also be clues in the clothes they were wearing and how old they looked. Pretty young. It was definitely a few years ago, and consid- ering she'd been murdered ten years ago, that made sense.

I turned back to face the kitchen. That young woman was gorgeous. Her long hair was up in a ponytail, her pale skin was blemish free, and her smile revealed straight, white teeth. His hair was dark brown—much darker than it was now. Was that his natural colour, or had he dyed it? I filed that question away for later.

In and of itself, the scene wasn't unusual and didn't prove anything, except that he had dated the woman I'd seen at the stream.

"Lily, we're going to cut the cake now." Marcia tapped my shoulder.

I started and lowered my camera. "Oh, great. I have to say, I love what you've done with this room. It's gorgeous." I smiled.

"I wanted it to be magical." She winked and smiled.

"Oh, and happy birthday." I couldn't believe I'd forgotten. That was the whole reason I was here. Dur.

She laughed. "Thank you! Now it's time to get this done so I can toast with another glass of champers." She turned around and held her hand up. My scalp tingled a fraction of a second before a large black-handled knife flew from the cake table to her hand, and a glass of champagne appeared in her other hand. Um... okay. A few of the family laughed. They must be used to drunken displays of magic. I wasn't sure it was such a good idea. Did the PIB have rules for using magic when over the limit? I mean, it made sense to have some kind of legal boundaries. I would definitely put "making knives fly through the air" on the list of offences.

She stumbled on her way to the other side of the table,

and her brother grabbed her arm, steadying her. "We want you to make it to your eighty-first birthday, love." He laughed, and she giggled. Oh brother.

Jeremy met my gaze from the other side of the dining table. He smirked and shook his head. I'm glad someone else thought Marcia was a tad out of control. I returned his smirk in kind. Was I being duped? Was he actually a nice guy, incapable of serial murder, or any murder, for that matter? Why couldn't James just call him in for an interview and get Beren to read his mind?

Everyone sang "Happy Birthday," and I snapped away as Marcia managed to blow out her candles—it took four goes—and cut the cake without maiming anyone. We all cheered, and I took some pics of Marcia laughing while one of her older granddaughters cut the cake into pieces and placed them on plates. Mmm, cake. The icing may have been white, but the inside was all chocolate. My stomach grumbled. *Shhhh. Don't embarrass me. It's not our party.*

Jeremy stepped up to the table to get some cake. He took two pieces, turned, and smiled. "Would you like some cake, Lily?"

"Oh, ah… but I'm working."

"Gran will be upset if you don't have any. You're practically family now you've seen most of our dirty laundry." He laughed and held the cake out to me.

Gah, there was no way I could refuse the sweet tendrils of chocolatey goodness wafting up my nose. Saliva burst into my mouth. "If you insist. It's too hard to say no to chocolate cake." I let my camera hang around my neck, took the plate, and spooned spongy cake into my mouth. "Mmm, this is so good."

He grinned, chocolate cake stuck on his tooth so it looked like his tooth was missing. I laughed and pointed at it. "What?"

"Hobo."

"What?" He laughed.

"You have cake smeared all over your teeth."

He closed his mouth, then opened it and showed me his teeth. "Better?"

"Yep. You have all your teeth again. Your gran has good taste in cakes. This is delicious." I ate more.

"She does. And she has great taste in photographers."

Damn. Why did he have to go and do that? "Ah, thanks." My cheeks heated again. "I'm sure you don't mean anything by that except we all have great taste, but I do have a boyfriend, and I'm not comfortable flirting with someone else." Oh my God. Talk about awkward. Had I just assumed he was flirting? How embarrassing. What if I'd gotten it wrong, and he was just being nice?

"Of course I don't mean anything by it. You and my gran definitely have great taste in all things, I'm sure." He winked. "Sorry if I overstepped the line. I'm just used to women flirting with me, and I think it's like an automatic thing for me to flirt back." His eyes widened. "Not that I thought you were flirting with me. You're just so easy to talk to. I feel comfortable around you, which doesn't happen often. Anyway, I'm not trying anything on. Promise. I think I like that you're *not* flirting with me." He grinned. So disarming. Stupid good-looking man that he was. Okay, so he wasn't stupid. Is this how he reeled in his victims—all charm and a bit of spice? Hmm.

I pushed my thoughts away and smiled. "Thanks. Sorry for making it uncomfortable. I just didn't want any misunderstandings."

"It's all good."

Standing a few feet away, scowling at us, was his mother. She narrowed her eyes, obviously trying to tell me something not very nice. Sheesh. She was so overprotective. If she were a magpie, she'd be pecking my eyes out by now.

My phone dinged with a message. Was it finally Will? I placed my plate on the table and fished my phone out of my pocket. It was him. *Hi, it's me. Can we talk?*

I swallowed as my stomach free-fell to the ground and splatted. That question had long sparked fear in the hearts of millions. *I'm at work. I'm not sure what time I'll finish. Do you want me to text you when I'm done?* I resisted adding, *Are you breaking up with me?* at the end. If he wasn't, I'd look way too needy. Bloody relationship politics. Why couldn't I let my insecurities out? Everyone had them. Why did others think it meant the person was needier? Needier sounded silly. Was it really a word? I thought it was.

"Lily, are you okay?" Jeremy was staring at me.

"Oh, ah, yeah. I was just wondering if needier was a word."

He drew his brows down momentarily, then burst out laughing.

"I know I'm weird." I shrugged, and he nodded, but his

smile suggested it was far from a bad thing. Gah, not now, cute movie star. Not now. My phone dinged again. "I just have to reply to this message."

"Jeremy, darling, can you help me with something please?" His mother had closed in, and I was actually happy about it. I could do with some space. What if Will's message made me cry? Was he still in love with Dana? Was he sick of me already? Surely not sick of *me*. I snorted in spite of myself. I was awesome. If he didn't like me anymore, that was his problem. Yep, I knew how to put on a brave face, but I wasn't fooling anyone, and by *anyone*, I meant me. *Nice try, Lily.*

Jeremy excused himself and followed his mother into the kitchen. I looked down at my phone. *No, that's fine. It can wait until tomorrow. I have to be at work early, but text me when you're up, and I'll pop in.* Right, so I wasn't getting any sleep tonight.

Yeah, sure. I would've put a smiley face on it, but I didn't feel like pretending, even in messaging. And he hadn't signed it with "Your Crankypants." I blinked back the scalding moisture I always seemed to have on tap. I was as efficient as an instantaneous gas hot-water system. Yay me.

A particularly loud cackle reverberated over all other noise. Back to reality. I was supposed to be working and finding clues. Right. I shoved all thoughts of Will aside—okay, not *all* thoughts, but most of them—and lifted my camera up to focus on the kids who were gleefully enjoying their cake.

I infused my voice with happiness I didn't feel. "Hey, kids, look this way. And... smile!"

CHAPTER 6

After tossing and turning and agonising all night, I finally fell asleep at around 4:00 a.m. When I awoke at nine, I groaned. I wasn't ready to get up. Hmm, maybe I could sleep in another hour—I wasn't due at Marcia's family lunch until twelve. But there was no way I could go back to sleep. If I didn't get up and face Will now, I'd have to wait until tonight, or possibly tomorrow, and I didn't want another day of stressing about what ifs. There was a chance he wouldn't dump me, small as it might be.

Clinging onto that tiny lifebuoy called chance, I made it out of bed. Normally, I dressed the human way, but today I didn't have the energy, so I magicked my PJs off, then my clothes on. I was back in black—black straight-leg jeans, long-sleeve black shirt, black knee-length boots, and black fitted jacket. Why didn't I dress with magic every day? It was so much easier, especially when it was cold. There was no racing to get covered while freezing. I needed to more fully embrace my witchiness.

I used the toilet—because, let's face it, who didn't wake up busting to go—then reluctantly grabbed my iPhone off my bedside table and went downstairs to have my coffee and message Will. As I haltingly traversed one step after the other, I imagined someone yelling, "Dead woman walking!" When you died, others mourned, but when only part of you died, you were the sole person grieving, and no one could really share your pain. Life sucked.

Or maybe I was overreacting.

As I approached the kitchen, I magicked a cappuccino into life, so it was waiting for me by the time I sat at the table. It was just me and the coffee. As much as I loved coffee, it wasn't as much of a comfort as it normally was. I could've done with my bestie sitting here, but her chair was empty. I breathed in the melancholy until I was drowning in it. What would my mother have said if she were here? Probably to stop wallowing and just message Will. That I was worrying for most likely nothing, but even if the thing I feared the most happened, I would get through it. I always had, and I always would.

"You'd be right, Mum," I said quietly. "Miss you." I sniffed back my tears and texted Will. *I'm in the kitchen having my coffee if you want to come over.* I pressed Send and sighed. Whatever was about to happen would not be worse than losing my parents. I might cry and have weeks or months of crappy days, but I would, eventually, be happy again.

I'll be there soon. At least I hadn't had to wait all day for an answer.

I sipped my coffee and ignored my roiling stomach.

"Hey."

I jumped and sloshed coffee over the sides of my cup. Damn quiet witches. It dribbled onto my hand, and I licked it off before turning around. My breath caught. His grey-blue eyes were serious but as sexy as ever, and the dimple when he smiled almost made me sigh. Hang on... he was smiling.

"Hey, yourself. What's going on?" My light, casual tone gave nothing away. He looked happy to see me, which had to mean he wasn't here to declare he could never get over Piranha. But I'd reserve my right to breathe when I knew for sure.

He cocked his head to the side and opened his arms. "Is that any kind of greeting for the man of your dreams?" He smirked.

I so wanted to punch him right now, but my hormones won, and I jumped up and into his embrace. I breathed in the clean-shirt scent he was currently sporting and revelled in the relief that cascaded over me. His arms tightened around me, and he rested his cheek on my head. "I missed you, Lily. Sorry I couldn't talk to you about this earlier. I've just had a lot of thinking to do."

"I've missed you too." I didn't want to go into my own

insecurities right now. He didn't need to know the depressing depths to which my imagination dragged me. Plus, he had his own real stuff to work through. I looked up at him. "So…."

He smiled. "I would like a kiss first. Then we can talk."

"It's like that, is it?"

"Yep." He lowered his lips to mine. Mmm….

When we were done, we sat at the table. "Coffee or tea?" I asked.

"I just had a coffee, so, no thanks." He grabbed my hand and held it. This was so much better than what I thought was going to happen today. "Anyway, I was shocked when I saw the photos, partly because I wasn't expecting to see Dana again, and also because it brought so many questions to mind."

"Other than what the hell do her parents have to do with everything and why were they eating with my parents, what questions did you have?"

"Okay. Why don't we start there? But hang on a sec." He waggled the fingers of his free hand. "Bubble of silence activated." He grinned. It really was crazy and reminded me of the old TV show *Get Smart*. My parents used to watch the reruns on TV. "What conclusions did you come to, Lily?"

"Well, either my parents are part of this crazy snake group, or they were trying to infiltrate it and take it down. Or, maybe her parents were with the PIB, and my parents happened to be their friends and had no idea of any rogue group. My money is on the last two choices. I can't imagine they'd do anything illegal, and I know they weren't power hungry." The need to discuss this with James tugged at me. "Should we organise a meeting for tomorrow? I've got this photography job on from lunchtime to whenever. I'd really like to get James and Angelica's takes on it."

"You've come to the three conclusions I'd come to. I never actually met her parents in all the time we dated. She told me they didn't get along, and she didn't want to see them, so I left it alone. I've done some preliminary investigation, but very quietly because we've found two agents we think are connected to Dana and her group." I must have pulled a face... okay, I had pulled a face, because he said, "I want you to know that I have no pleasant feelings towards her whatsoever. We're definitely history. She's not the person I thought she was, and even if she was a little bit who I thought she was, she doesn't hold a candle to you, Lily."

The way he gazed at me. Sigh. My cheeks heated, and my skin tingled. No one had ever had this effect on me. He leaned in and kissed me again. Eventually I leaned back, a goofy grin in place. "I needed to hear that. And no one has ever made me feel the way you do, Will. I like you... a lot." Gah, I hated being sappy, but the words wanted out—I had no choice.

"The feeling is mutual." He rubbed the top of my hand with his thumb. If he didn't stop being so lovable, I was going to do something I may or may not regret—we were home alone, after all.

I cleared my throat. "Um, maybe we should get back to

talking? You're dressed for work, and I'm assuming we don't have that long?"

He laughed. "You would assume correctly. Maybe next weekend you can come stay at my place?"

My mouth formed a medium-sized *O*. That was something I had not expected.

"No pressure, Lily. I mean, we don't have to *do* anything if you're not ready. I just thought it would be awesome to spend the whole weekend together. What do you think?"

I laughed. "Um, no, I wasn't worried about *that*. I just wasn't expecting it. I would love to accept your invitation." He grinned. We were good. Thank God. "Now that's sorted, can you tell me if you know for sure those two PIB agents are working for Dana and her crew?"

"We haven't gotten hard evidence—proof that they've spoken to or met with her lately, but they were both in close contact with her when she worked for us, and one of them has the same tattoo. Beren saw it the other day when they were on an undercover assignment. The other guy may have a similar tattoo, but we haven't had the opportunity to see him without full PIB gear on. Both agents don't spend much time together at work, but we've discovered their Facebook aliases, and they're friends on there and often comment on each other's posts."

"You're relying on Facebook statuses to confirm they're friends? Wow, talk about desperate." I sniggered.

"That's what you do if you don't want to be caught snooping. We don't know what they're tracking at the bureau—phones, computers, whether they've bugged offices. Dana's probably infiltrated PIB systems somewhere. They may know what we search online and what we don't. We bought burner phones to search. Those guys catch up at least once a week outside of work. We've put a tail on them, but it's not easy since they're agents. It's a rather delicate operation. We're keeping tabs on everyone they meet with."

"Fair enough. Sorry. Just… Facebook and real spying seems funny. I guess Facebook spies on us for marketing purposes anyway; what's the difference if the PIB is using it to find stuff out? Other government departments probably do too. They're always listening in. Bastards. Does the bubble of silence encompass mobile phones? Our phones are in the bubble." Oh, crap. How had I never considered that before?

He half laughed. "Don't worry. Our phones are in the bubble, but they can only transmit as far as the bubble, so nothing actually gets through to anyone else. As if we wouldn't have thought of that, Lily. We're not idiots, and this is definitely not *Get Smart*."

I blinked and checked my mind-shield. Nope, all good— it was up. If I didn't know better, I would have said he'd been listening to my thoughts, but maybe we were just really in tune? "Thanks for the confirmation. I do wonder some-times." I grinned.

He rolled his eyes. "Have I told you lately what a pita you are?"

Huh? "A flat piece of Greek bread?"

Will smirked. "No: a Pain in the Arse."

"No, but thank you. I do try." I stuck my tongue out in a

show of great maturity. "But seriously, what now? There must be something my camera and I can do to figure out more. I need to know what my parents were really doing. Do you think Angelica knows anything?"

He shrugged. "We'll have to ask her. Like I said, we'll get a meeting set up, and everyone can be there to contribute. I think we need to go through your mum's diary and pick out more places we can go and grab some pictures from. What do you think?"

As much as it hurt to see them through the lens, it hurt even more not knowing what happened to them. The tiny niggle that they may have been voluntarily involved in something underhanded prodded me, but I ignored it: these were my parents we were talking about, and I knew them, knew they weren't capable of being criminals.

Didn't I?

WILL SPOKE TO ANGELICA, AND THEY SET UP A MEETING AT James's for the following evening. Then he kissed me goodbye and went to work, leaving me with a couple of hours until I had to be at Marcia's lunch.

Not wanting to go crazy harping on my parents and Dana, I got back to editing Marcia's photos. The two hours flew by, and before I knew it, I was driving to Marcia's lunch. They were having it at an old pub about six miles west of Westerham. In typical English style, it was a quaint two-storey building, whitewashed, and a tad lopsided. The thatched roof reminded me of a bad toupee.

The interior had low ceilings. Thick beams reached across the expanse, hovering mere inches above me. My head didn't touch the roof, but I ducked anyway, then had to force myself to stand straight. I walked past a bar and to a large, timber-floored dining area brimming with noise: Marcia and her family. Jeremy spied me first and hurried over.

"Hey, photo lady." He grinned his movie-star smile.

"Hey, movie guy." I grinned in return.

"Someone's happy today."

The stress of not knowing whether Will wanted me or not had floated off into the ether. It was wonderful to have one less thing to worry about. "Yep. I had stuff happening, but it's all sorted. I feel much better today. How is everyone? Is Marcia still enjoying herself?"

"Always. Come on." He turned and led the way to his family.

As soon as Marcia saw me, she gave me a hug. "Lovely to see you again, Lily."

"Lovely to see you too. How does it feel to be eighty?"

"Absolutely marvellous." She grinned and fist-pumped the air. I giggled. She was such a character. In keeping with that, she wore a fuchsia shirt with angel-style sleeves. At least I think that's what they were called. They were flowy sleeves that almost touched her knees. Or were they more like priest-robe sleeves? Meh, whatever. They were huge sleeves. Her black trousers toned the look down somewhat, but then she partied things up with mirrorball-style court shoes. I squinted. Yep, there really were tiny little mirrors all over them.

Jeremy's mother sauntered over. "So… you're back."

"That was the plan, Catherine." Marcia rolled her eyes at her daughter. "Not everyone is trying to take advantage of your son. Leave the poor young lady alone. She's an incredible photographer. You should see her work."

Ooh, a compliment. I never said no to one of those. "Thank you, Marcia."

"Well, it's true. I looked up so many websites, and your shots were the best. So much atmosphere, and I loved your clean style."

Catherine folded her arms. "Oh, just wait. She'll probably sell photos of my Jeremy to the magazines when this is all over. She'll use it somehow. Just watch."

Ah, excuse me? I was about to open my mouth and say exactly that when Jeremy stood between his mother and me. "I trust Lily. She's not here to get famous. Not everyone wants that, Mother."

"Oh, yes, they do. Don't be so naïve." Catherine took her two fingers, pointed them at her own eyes and then at me, in the universal sign for "I'm watching you." Was she kidding? What were we, twelve? Or were we in some C-grade movie? Jeremy shook his head, exasperation permeating from his whole body. I pitied him. He didn't have it all like I'd initially thought. He had a great career and many adoring fans, but he didn't have someone who truly loved him, and his mother was a total b—

"Gran! Gran! Come and see! Bailey's caught a centipede."

Hmm, that kind of rhymed. Oh, and so did that! I snorted. Jeremy gave me a perplexed look, then smiled, and his mother just glared. Oh well. Can't please everyone.

"Here, let me help you." Jeremy took the heavy bag off my shoulder. "Where do you want this?"

"Just over there, next to the wall and out of the way. Thanks." He was such a nice guy… or was he? I needed to figure this out before I went crazy second-guessing it. Oscillating back and forth was doing my head in. The question that did pop up, now that I considered it, was how come no one had been murdered lately? If you're a serial killer, you aren't doing a great job if you stop at three. Maybe the killer was already in jail for something else so was out of action? Or maybe the killer had died or become disabled and wasn't able to carry on his spree?

I unfolded my tripod and found a great spot to set it up. I had a clear view down the long line of table, which was set for what was going to be a yummy lunch—not that I was actually having any. There were two sets of knives and forks, a set of dessertspoons and forks, and side plates. Looked as if everyone would be rolling out of here totally satisfied. A waiter balancing a large tray offered glasses of champagne, and the mouth-watering aroma of garlic bread enveloped me. Would they let me have a piece? *No, Lily. You're on the job.*

But I need it, my stomach wailed. I sniffed deeper. Oh, the travesty.

I swallowed all that extra saliva. *Sorry, stomach. I'll get you some for dinner. Promise.*

"You can't go in there. It's a private party!" a woman's distressed voice came from the entry. I turned.

A man with a large, shoulder-mounted video camera hurried after a taller man who held a microphone. "Jeremy, we just need to ask you a few questions." He barged his way through Jeremy's family to reach him. How rude. I hurriedly turned on my camera and started shooting my own video. Maybe Jeremy could do with proof later that these guys had stormed in and accosted him.

Jeremy's jaw set. "Get out! You can't just crash my grandmother's birthday celebrations." His fists were tight at his sides, and it looked like he was doing all he could to remain calm. The public would eat up another celebrity-behaving-badly moment. "Please leave."

"Not until we get a statement from you. You don't look too upset."

His brow wrinkled. "What? About you barging in here? Trust me; I'm upset."

"No. Tell us, Jeremy, are you even a little sad that your fiancé's been murdered?"

Jeremy's mouth dropped open, as did pretty much his entire family's. Why would they bring up his girlfriend's old murder? And I'd thought they were only dating and not yet engaged.

Marcia scrambled to reach him and put a comforting hand on his arm. She glared at the duo. "Leave now, please. This is no place for any such discussion." As old as she was, right then, she looked like a mamma bear protecting her cubs—fierce and not to be messed with. Her voice was strong and brooked no argument. The media guys exchanged glances, neither knowing what call to make.

Sirens whined in the distance. The manager must have called them as soon as the news guys burst in. Still, had the police been driving past? Unless they could witch travel, that was pretty damn quick.

"I suggest you leave now or risk being arrested," the manager said, her hands on her hips.

"How do you know they're not random police cars that are going to drive past? Huh?" The guy with the microphone raised his brows. "I didn't see you call them."

The manager locked eyes with Marcia and shrugged. Had she called them? If not her, then who?

The sirens became deafening, then shut off as three cars skidded to a halt in the pub parking lot. I was still filming—might as well see where this went. I panned across to Jeremy, his mother, and the rest of the family. Everyone was ping-ponging their gazes from Jeremy, to the manager, to the reporter, and out the small windows to the approaching police. Jeremy's brow creased, and his mother shook her head at him, as if chastising him. What was that about?

The police strode in—six of them. The biggest one, at around six foot six, and with an officer on either side of him, approached Jeremy. "Are you Jeremy Alfred Frazer?"

Jeremy's eyes were wide. He nodded, then managed to stammer, "Y—yes, sir. I'm Jeremy."

"Turn around, son. You're under arrest for suspicion of

murdering Trudie Fawn Allen. You do not have to say anything—"

Catherine screamed, "My baby!" She fainted to the floor, landing with a loud thud.

"But I didn't do anything. I didn't do it!" Jeremy had paled.

His grandmother put her hand on his shoulder. "Of course you didn't. I believe you."

Jeremy's brother stood toe to toe with one of the officers, who said, "Please step aside, both of you, or you'll be arrested for hindering an arrest."

Marcia's gaze darkened, and the resonance of power zinged down my spine. My eyes widened. I lowered my camera and shook my head at her. "Marcia, I think it's a good idea to do what the officer's asked. We'll get to the bottom of this. I promise." Gah, there I went, making promises I couldn't keep to stop a situation devolving into violence. And whatever happened would be caught on camera and probably be on the national news tonight. He might have been guilty, so we'd all be safer with him behind bars, and it wouldn't do for the general public to find out about witches and magic. That would be a whole other headache, and I really didn't want to see Marcia arrested— the PIB would be sure to come down on her hard if she hindered an arrest with magic.

Marcia looked at me, her brow furrowed as she likely assessed how I was going to get to the bottom of anything. She didn't move or say a word, and the essence of power lingered, warming my skin. She obviously was not convinced.

I nodded towards the news guys, looked back at her and raised a brow, then tried again. "What good can you do for Jeremy if you're in jail? There's going to be enough on the news tonight as it is." I gritted my teeth, as if the force of my jaw could make her get what I was saying—no magic in public.

"Listen to the young lady. She's making a lot of sense. Now please, move aside, all of you." The officer turned, shoving Jeremy around, pointing him in the direction of the exit. Jeremy's gaze darted from the officers to his grand-mother, brother, and then mother, who was now sitting up and being comforted by other family members. As they pushed him out the door and bulbs flashed from the awaiting paparazzi, he turned back to give me one last look. The emotion in his eyes could only be described as "help me!"

I ran to the door. Some guy was jogging alongside and shouting at Jeremy as the police took him to the car. "I've been waiting a long time for this. If you hadn't stolen Amanda from me, none of this would have happened. Karma, baby. Enjoy jail, Frazer."

A niggle tapped on my brain. That's where I'd seen him before! It was the balding guy with the earring from the pap crowd at Marcia's yesterday. So, had Jeremy stolen Amanda from him? Even if he had, surely he should have gotten over it by now? Had he killed Amanda as payback to both her and him—the old if-I-don't-get-to-have-her-you-can't-either thing. Had he known about Jeremy's stalker from yesterday? Maybe she magicked herself into town, and he recognised her. Or maybe Jeremy was a killer and an evil girlfriend stealer.

The guy spat at Jeremy as the police put him in one of their cars, press closing in on all sides like seagulls descending on scraps, squawking and flapping, trying to pick at their share of the hot chips. This would all be on TV tonight, and it would likely spread way further than UK shores. I frowned. That had been... intense, and the violence of it all made me shudder.

I needed to find out what evidence they had on him. I still had doubts he would be capable of doing something like that. And I had to know whether we should keep looking for the murderer because if they'd arrested the wrong person, obviously more dead bodies would continue turning up. But was it really my place? And I had more important things to investigate, like my parents' disappearance.

The paparazzi shouted as the car drove off, and they ran after it. Idiots.

But then one pap, the only one who hadn't run, a chubby guy with particularly heavy-looking camera equipment, turned to me. "Hey, how does it feel to be related to a murderer? Did you know he was a murderer? Are you an accessory?" The photographers heard him, and then, they were all jogging towards me in a frenzy of shutter clicks.

"Oh, crap." I jumped inside and slammed the door. My preference was to be on the other side of the camera.

Shouting outside and crying inside. Marcia was hugging Jeremy's brother and sobbing. Jeremy's mother stared out one of the small windows, her face slack with what I suspected was shock. Everyone else looked at each other, and no one spoke louder than a whisper. It must be time for me to go home.

The party was definitely over.

CHAPTER 7

Olivia shook her head while staring at our TV, watching the nightly news. "I can't believe you haven't gotten me an autograph yet. He's going to be even more famous after this." Images of Jeremy visiting sick kids in hospital played behind the newsreader, then a clip of him feeding a baby goat with a bottle. Then, to show how far he'd fallen, on came the scrimmage of photographers jostling him this afternoon as he was led to the police car and shoved in, all semblance of pride gone. And there was the guy with the earring, shouting, then lunging at Jeremy and spitting. Ew, that was the moment I'd seen yesterday.

Olivia leaned forward, her dark eyes wide. "Oh, my word, it's you, Lily. You're on TV!"

Out of everything we'd just seen, *that* was what she picked up on? Argh, just great. There I was, deer in headlights, practically throwing myself back through the door to the event venue and slamming it shut. That was just before I had decided to leave, but then I'd been stuck there for another thirty minutes until more police came and cleared a path through the vultures hoping to get a comment from the family. They were trespassing, being on the grounds, so the manager had them removed... finally.

Olivia turned to me. "You looked great! You're so photogenic."

"Um, thanks." That was debatable, especially when I had my stunned-mullet expression happening.

Then a picture of the murdered woman came on screen, and disappointment sat uncomfortably in my stomach like undercooked chicken from an all-you-can-eat place. "Oh, wow. It's the woman from yesterday, the one who turned up saying they were married." The newsreader was saying they were engaged, and that after telling her family she was joining Jeremy for his grandmother's celebrations, she wasn't answering her phone. They didn't have Jeremy's number and called local police, who had found her body, although they weren't saying where. A photo of them from two years ago popped up. They were facing the camera on a red carpet, arms around each other, and smiling. He'd been trying to avoid her for years, he'd said, but there they were—together. This did not look good.

"So, what do you think, Liv? Is he guilty?" Maybe asking her was a waste of time because she'd been a fan of his for so long, but I was pretty sure she could put her police hat on and look at it objectively.

The news changed to the next story about the rise in train fares. I grabbed the remote and switched the TV off. "So, Liv. Tell me."

She shrugged. "I don't know. He doesn't look guilty. He's so handsome and nice. I mean, I just can't imagine him killing anyone. Can you?"

"I have no idea. I can't, really, but then, isn't that a good trait for a serial killer—the ability to appear innocent? How many times have you heard people say they just couldn't believe their next-door neighbour or brother or childhood friend or whatever had killed their wife? He lied about being with that woman, but he just looked so forlorn. Wouldn't you think a serial killer would be angry or something because they believe they're above reproach? They might even look happy because they're going to be famous. But then, he was already famous, so he doesn't fit that particular profile."

"I don't know. Maybe? And before, about the auto-graph, I was only joking. What if he really did it? I'm going to have to get used to hating him."

"But we don't know, and it's not our job to find out, unless someone asks us, of course."

She raised a brow. "You mean the PIB?"

"Well, he is a witch. I imagine they're going to be inves-tigating it."

"But do you have time, what with the meeting tomorrow night and following up on those you-know-what people?"

She meant the snake group, and lucky for me, she had the presence of mind not to say their name out loud because I hadn't put up a bubble of silence. I swore that one day I was going to get the hang of being a witchy spy person, but I guessed that was why I forgot stuff—it wasn't my full-time job, and it never would be. I just wanted to take photographs. Although that hadn't worked out too well this weekend. What a shambles. This was an eightieth birthday Marcia, her family, and I were unlikely to forget.

"Not much time, no. I suppose we just leave it up to James and the crew. That's what they're there for."

"And me." She grinned.

"But of course. How could I forget? James has said you're a massive asset. You've found your calling, methinks."

She grinned. "I really feel like I have. My parents weren't happy at first—policing isn't exactly the safest or happiest of jobs—but it's not like I'm out in the field amongst danger. Research and administration are what I love, and Millicent's been getting me to read through evidence and tell her what I think. She says I have a knack for seeing what others miss."

I smiled. "That doesn't surprise me. I'm so happy it's all worked out." After her fiancé cheated on her and was killed in a shootout with the PIB while trying to kill me, she'd had a rough time. She'd moved out of home and changed jobs, and now everything was going the way it should. Now she and Beren just had to get their acts together, and all would be perfect.

"So, you're not going to look into it?"

I shook my head. "It's not my place, and besides, they must have some good evidence if they've arrested him—you don't do that to someone so famous unless you're pretty damn sure. Imagine if they got it wrong? The public is already calling for them to release him. Have you seen Twitter and Facebook?"

"Can't say I have. I'm more of an Insta girl."

"Well, there's a trending hashtag 'ReleaseJeremy.' I'd hate to be the person who okayed his arrest if he's eventually proven innocent."

"I hope he's not the killer. I still have a mini-crush on him from *Seven Steps to Heaven*. He made such a sexy angel."

As much as I wasn't into fangirling over people, I had to concede, he had looked good in that one, and his character had been just the right mix of take charge, romantic, and not at all creepy. "Yeah, I suppose he did. But that's not reality. You know that, right?" I smirked.

She chucked a throw pillow at me. It glanced my head as I dodged to the side. Well, throw pillows were for throwing. No one could blame her. "I don't think he's that great an actor, to be honest. I think some of them tend to play the same characters over and over because that's who they kind of are. So, I think he really is a nice person and a bit of a cad because that's who he always plays."

I looked at her, unsure of my previous opinion of her high intelligence. It was true—he could be a really nice cad…. "Or… he's a really good actor." I laughed. "Anyway, it's not up to us, and if he is a serial killer, he's definitely *not* a nice person, and you'll need to get over it. I'm totally staying away from the whole thing. Anyway, enough talk of Jeremy. What are we doing for dinner?"

"Hmm, what abou—"

My phone rang, cutting her off. I looked at the screen. Angelica. "Hi. What's up?"

"Hello, dear. I didn't really want to call you, but I have no choice." Her voice was businesslike and firm, so I didn't think it was going to be terrible news, but I sat up straighter, worried about why she was calling.

"Have no choice about what?" I asked. Olivia looked at me questioningly. I shrugged.

"After the police took Jeremy to their facilities, James contacted them, and he was moved here. Seems there was no one on duty who knew about witches or us, and they cuffed him with normal cuffs, which does happen from time to time, but if he was thinking of going rogue, he could easily have escaped. We're lucky he's not violent."

"But if he killed the woman they say he did, doesn't that mean he is violent?"

"Killing a helpless woman in private is different to attacking male police officers in front of multiple cameras. There would be no point trying to escape. With his career, it would be hard for him to hide anywhere. Everyone knows who he is, and he'd never blend in somewhere he wasn't famous, like Cambodia."

"Okay, fair enough. So, what did you have to tell me?" I didn't do suspense well. My knee jiggled up and down like a super-caffeinated hummingbird, and I suppressed a huge sigh.

"Jeremy's got himself a solicitor—one of the best, actually—and she's asked to meet with you. You're going to be one of their star witnesses, apparently."

"What?" I wrinkled my brow. "But I hardly know him. And why wouldn't the solicitor contact me directly? Why go through you?"

"When I said she was one of the best, I wasn't joking. She's done her due diligence and discovered you're living with one of the most senior PIB investigators and that you're the sister of another one. She asked me to call you, said she was doing that as a favour to the PIB." If anyone's tone could convey an eye-roll over the phone, it was Angelica's. "Jeremy must think you'd vouch for him. Any reason he'd think that, Lily?"

I blinked. Even though I was speaking to Angelica, and this was likely not admissible in court, I didn't want to say too much. I might accidentally condemn an innocent man, or I might help set a criminal free. My gut feeling was that I liked him, and we got along well, but I hardly knew him. I finally let out the sigh that had been threatening for the past couple of minutes. "No. I was nice to him and everyone at the birthday I was photographing for, well, except maybe his mother. She was hard work. I'm assuming you know all about how Jeremy and I know each other?"

"But of course."

"Well, that's all I can say. Now what happens?"

"I'll text you her details. She's a witch, of course. Her name's Florence Peters. If you could give her a call in the morning and go from there. And you don't have to see them, but if they think you're important enough, they can subpoena you and force you to be a witness, although that won't be conducive to having you do what they want."

"Are you suggesting they'll ask me to perjure myself? Because I won't."

She sighed. "No, Lily. Not really, but just be careful. And you won't be able to tell anyone what you speak about with them. If you do, you could jeopardise our case against him. Understood?"

Man, everyone was going to be in a sticky situation—all because I happened to be the photographer in the wrong place at the wrong time. Why did I always get caught up in stuff? It was as if I were a crime magnet. I seemed to find crimes when all I was looking for were cappuccinos, double-chocolate muffins, and pretty landscapes to photograph. "Yes, Ma'am. I'll call her in the morning, and I won't discuss it with anyone." Olivia raised her brows at that.

"Not even Olivia, Lily. I'm serious."

How the hell did she know? I rolled my eyes and shook my head at Liv. "Not even Olivia."

"Or Will."

"Or Will, or James, or Millicent, or their dogs. Is that everyone?"

"Ha ha, very funny, dear. I have to go now. But I'll text you those details. I'll be home in an hour or so."

"Okay. See you later." The call ended.

"What can't you discuss with me?" Olivia had a folder in her arms, a disbelieving expression on her face.

"Jeremy's case. Apparently his solicitor's calling me as a witness for their side. I won't be able to discuss anything with anyone." I pouted. That was going to be beyond difficult. My friends and family were the ones I bounced ideas and thoughts off. How was I going to figure this out on my own?

Liv leaned over and rubbed my arm. "It's okay, Lily. I'm not happy about it, but I can see you're not either. It'll be okay. You'll figure it out, and I promise I won't make it harder for you." She smirked. "My questions will remain unasked."

I smiled. "Thanks, Liv. Gah, this whole thing sucks. I only hope when all this is finished, justice is served." That wasn't too much to ask. Was it?

CHAPTER 8

Florence Peters worked for Evans and Peters Lawyers in a historic home just outside Westerham's main centre. It had the coolest name: Wolfelands House. That was a building you'd expect a witch to work in, and maybe a werewolf, if such things existed. And yes, I saw the irony in that statement.

I'd borrowed Angelica's car to get there. The three-storey red-brick building wasn't that far from the main high street, which was, incidentally, called High Street. It was just down the hill, on the A25. I could have run there in a few minutes, but I didn't think turning up sweaty and gross was the way to approach things. Still, I felt guilty driving such a short distance.

I sat in the carpeted waiting room, all sound muted as if the hushed conversations behind closed doors were about life and death, conspiracies and plots. It was if the air was heavier in here. I pushed back further into my chair, the feeling of inferiority making me want to be smaller and less noticeable. I glanced at the door. But that hope was useless. If I didn't do this willingly, I'd be dragged into it anyway, and I'd just stress the whole time while waiting for it to happen. Might as well get it over and done with.

My gaze flicked to the cream-coloured walls and the reproductions of famous artworks lining them: the *Mona Lisa* hung next to a portrait of Churchill seated and sternly observing me from on high. The more pleasant Monet's *Water Lilies*, and his *Rouen Cathedral* hung on the wall next to the door. What a dark, gothic place Rouen Cathedral appeared. It was in France. I should really pop over there and check it out. Maybe I could convince Will to come with me in the next couple of weeks if work wasn't too busy.

"Miss Bianchi, Florence will see you now." The receptionist opened a door next to her desk. "Please follow me." She strode down a long hallway and stopped at the second door on the right. She entered before me. "Florence, here's Miss Bianchi."

Her glass-and-stainless-steel table was covered in neat piles of paper and a desktop computer. She stood when I came in. A few years older than me, but probably still only thirty, she was slightly taller than me and had chestnut-coloured shoulder-length hair that was straight and shiny. Her make-up was applied with perfection, and she had a pretty face with tawny-coloured eyes. Maybe she really was a wolf shifter or something. Nah, I was being silly. Wasn't I?

She held out her slender arm. "Lovely to meet you, Miss

Bianchi. You can call me Florence. Do you mind if I call you Lily? I like to keep things fairly casual. Makes it less intimidating."

I shook her hand and returned her smile. "That's fine. Thanks, Florence."

"Please sit." As we sat, the receptionist exited, the door clicking shut quietly after her. "You're probably wondering why I've called you in on behalf of my client, Jeremy Frazer."

"I suppose so. I mean, I don't know him well."

"That's okay. I will ask for your first impressions of him, but what I really want to know are the times you were working for his grandmother, and at what times you were aware of his whereabouts."

I raised my brows. "Are you establishing an alibi?"

She nodded. "Yes. Without divulging too much—I don't want to be seen to be leading you—the woman was murdered sometime between the time she left his grand-mother's house and breakfast the next morning. I do realise that you weren't there the whole time, but please confirm the times you were there where my client was visible."

I had a think and told her what I could remember. But what use could I be? There was so much time when I was at home asleep when he could have killed her. Unless they could pinpoint the exact minute of her death, that left a lot of time open. If everyone in his house was asleep, how could he have any kind of alibi? Especially being a witch, he could pop around quietly without anyone noticing he was gone. As I spoke, she typed.

"Okay, thank you. And what were your first impressions of my client?"

I smiled, remembering his greeting at my car and what assumptions I'd made. I'd been wrong about the person he appeared to be as the day wore on. "He was a bit flirty in the first few minutes but not creepy. I just figured he was a typical up-himself movie star. But after we went into his gran's house, he was polite and helpful. Actually, he offered to carry my heavy gear from the car. He showed me around the property, and we chatted about random things, including his childhood. He seemed relaxed and was good company, to be honest. My impression at that time was that he was nice enough and fairly normal."

"So, you weren't getting any aggressive vibes?"

"No."

"Did he say anything inappropriate or rude at any time?"

I bit my top lip. Hmm…. "Nope. Not that I can recall."

"And how was he with his family members?"

This could get him in trouble, make him look a bit aggressive, but maybe not. Who knew. Didn't everyone have that one family member who drove them to want to kill on occasion? Actually, I didn't have one of those. Okay, so scrap that. "He seemed to get along with everyone, especially his grandmother and brother, but his mother was another matter. She was overbearing, and he pushed back."

"In what way?" She tilted her head to the side, appearing casual, but was this an important question? It was as if she were trying too hard to seem nonchalant.

"Just verbally. And I don't think he overreacted. He just told her what he thought, although he did raise his voice a bit. But honestly, I couldn't blame him. She was annoying and not very nice."

"Was she not very nice to you?"

"Not really."

"So you'd have reason to be on his side when it came to his mother."

"Yes."

"Hmm." She focussed on her computer screen and typed. And what exactly did "Hmm" mean? Was it a hmm, unreliable witness, or hmm, interesting information to help my client? I swallowed. I almost felt as if I were in the witness box, and I didn't like it. Was that what she was going for? Maybe it would be easier if she could get someone in to just read my mind and be done with it. Although, then they'd see all my secrets, and that would be less than ideal.

"You can't order someone to have their mind read, can you?"

"No. If we could, there would be no point in going to trial."

"It would mean less income for you, but wouldn't it mean more justice?"

She laughed quietly. "Unfortunately, no. Have you ever heard of mind tampering?"

"Yes."

"Thoughts and memories can be implanted. It's not common because it's a skill only a few witches possess. It's one thing to implant a thought without someone knowing, but it's another entirely to hide your magic signature when you do it, and those memories and thoughts are not permanent—they fade in time, and much quicker than real, lived memories. It has something to do with how they're embedded. Embedding them with a spell is very different from the way your brain does it."

"Oh, okay." That was good to know. Although, if they could just rely on mind reading, a lot less time and money would be wasted, plus, the guilty would always go to jail. Oh well.

She asked me a few more questions and noted my answers. After around forty minutes, we were done... for now. "Lily, thank you for coming in today. This is just a preliminary interview. We'll have more to talk about in due course. Are there any other questions you'd like to ask before we wrap this up?"

I wasn't sure if I should care—what if he was the killer —but I couldn't help asking. "How's he doing?" I also wanted to ask if she thought he did it, but that was the dumbest question ever. As if she'd tell me she thought he had.

She frowned. "As well as can be expected. He'll be pleading innocent, of course. Now we just have to get our ducks in a row and prove it to a court." She stood. "Thank you for your time, Lily. If you think of anything else that might help us, or even something you think may not, let me know. We need to prepare for all the information that's out there."

"I will."

She came around her desk and shook my hand, then opened the door and smiled. "I'll be in touch." She stood aside as I walked into the corridor.

"Okay, great." *Not.* As I left, I looked at the receptionist and did that kind-of smile where you roll your lips in and show no teeth. It was an, "I wish I could smile, but there's nothing to smile about" mouth. My stomach gurgled, and not because it was hungry. It was an unsettled, unhappy growl. As confident and professional as the lawyer was, and even though Angelica had said she was one of the best, the universe was telling me bad things were coming Jeremy's way. I just wished I knew whether or not he deserved them.

Wanting to placate my stomach, at least a little bit, I stopped in at Costa and grabbed a cappuccino and double-chocolate muffin. Now that my magic skills were greatly improved and the PIB was short-staffed, I was allowed to do things without agents trailing me... that I knew of. I always kept an eye out, and I hadn't caught sight of any, but they were supposed to be good at covert operations. At least now I could enjoy outings without consulting everyone. Today, I wanted to eat in, so I sat in a window seat.

"Excuse me, miss."

I turned. An older man at the table behind me had tapped me on the shoulder. "Yes?"

"Did you know that a while ago, a car crashed through that window and killed an elderly lady?"

I blinked. Oooookay. "Um, no, actually. That's really sad."

He stared at me... waiting. For what, I wasn't sure. As I

turned to get back to my food, he said, "But, why aren't you moving?"

"Why would I move?"

"It's bad luck. What if another car comes crashing in?"

I wished Liv was here to share in this guy's idiocy. "Firstly, the chance of it happening once is pretty slim, and I imagine twice is near impossible. Secondly, you're sitting right behind me. If a car were to come crashing in here, it would probably take you out too." I smiled sweetly.

His eyes widened. His gaze snapped around to an elderly woman who sat opposite him. "We must move. Quick. Move." They stood as quickly as their aged bodies allowed and hurriedly shuffled to a table further back, out of the path of any wayward vehicles. I smirked as I turned to face the window and watch the world passing by.

What a crazy few months it had been. I smiled as I remembered the first time I'd come in here. The comforting warmth, freshly brewed coffee fragrance, and English-accented chatter had hit me like a massive tackle hug, and it still felt the same. I'd even met my best friend here. Liv no longer worked behind the counter, but she still enjoyed visiting and saying hi to her old workmates. This place felt like home. That hadn't taken long. I missed the beach and surf—it had been a huge part of my life—but I loved the oldness, history, and prettiness of the UK, and of course, my brother was here. It turned out that what had seemed a huge ask—moving to another country—hadn't been such a big deal after all. And it had brought me to Will.

A group of four teenage girls approached the door. They

must have been late teens because school was in, and they were out. They came in and made their way to the counter to order. The one with the brown ponytail said, "Do you think we'll catch a glimpse of him today?"

Her red-haired friend said, "I don't think so. Isn't he still in jail?"

The ponytail girl frowned. "Why didn't he get bail? He's, like, so famous. Surely they can't hold him in there too long."

The third friend, also brunette but sporting a short pixie cut, shook her head. "Didn't you hear? He's being charged with three more murders."

Their collective and loud intakes of breath smothered my own. Oh crap. They'd linked him to those other murders? Had that American woman the same type of wounds? This didn't bode well. I'd have to call James. Not that I could do anything.

Ponytail girl rolled her eyes. "Sheesh. Why did we come all this way then? I could've slept in. How are we supposed to celebrity watch if there aren't any celebrities out and about?" Hmm, her empathy centre was missing. I looked around at the other patrons. What if one of them was a friend or related to one of the murdered women? How would they feel? Thankfully, no one batted an eye.

The girls finished ordering and chose a table down the back, far away from me, so I was saved from having to listen to the rest of their conversation, but that extra bit of information sunk deep into my middle. Serial killer? Jeremy? I just couldn't picture it. Guilt lodged in my throat. I washed it down with coffee. Just because he was charismatic and attractive didn't mean he wasn't capable of murder, or even of enjoying murder. Was I blinded by those things? And if I was, shame on me. I shook my head to escape thoughts that followed the same track around and around. If I wasn't careful, I was going to create a whirlpool of misery and confusion that I wouldn't escape for the whole day.

Right. No more thinking about bad things. I again concentrated on the world passing by and thought of my awesome friends and family. While I munched my double-chocolate muffin, I counted my blessings. But no matter how much I tried to shift my focus, unease crept in. It couldn't leave me alone for five minutes. Sheesh. The problem was, I had no idea what the universe was trying to tell me.

But I needn't have worried. The universe made itself pretty clear soon enough.

CHAPTER 9

I travelled to James's reception room with Will and Liv. It was our fourth meeting about the Regula Pythonis- sam, or snake group as we affectionately called it. Okay, it wasn't because of affection—snake group was way easier to pronounce. Will had come to Angelica's first so we could have a decent smooch without an audience. Once we'd said our proper hellos, I grabbed Olivia, and we'd made our magical way to my brother's.

Millicent answered the door. Her normally small frame was still small but had the hugest beach-ball bump floating in front of it. She smiled, one hand on the doorframe and one on the small of her back. "Hey, everyone. How are we all?"

I leaned in, and we kissed each other's cheeks. "Not bad. What about you and my potential niece or nephew?"

"We're doing okay. The baby's so heavy now, though.

I'm having trouble getting around, and I don't fit at my PIB desk anymore." She laughed. Babies were kind of cute but carrying that stomach around wasn't. It looked the opposite of comfortable. Torture would be the word I was looking for.

She greeted Will and Liv, and we made our way to their dining-room-cum-substitute-meeting-room. The dogs' whining came from the back room where Mill had obviously locked them to keep them off Olivia, who had a phobia of large dogs.

"Hey, Beren!" I squished him in a big hug. It was still so good to see him alive and well. He'd died at his last big PIB assignment at a nursing home. James and I had done our best to save him, and we'd succeeded, thank God. But it had been way too close, and while I hadn't said it aloud, saving him had been nothing short of a miracle.

"How's my favourite witch? I saw you on TV earlier. Don't let the fame go to your head." He smirked.

I grinned. "Ha ha. Watch what you say, or I won't mention you in my Oscar's acceptance speech."

He laughed. "Will said you were there working. What's the goss? Do you think he did it?"

I shrugged. "I have no idea. He seems nice enough, and he doesn't give off any kind of serial-killer vibe."

"Serial killer?" Liv's eyes widened.

I turned to her. "I heard at Costa this afternoon. Apparently they're charging him with three other murders." I turned to James, who was standing behind a chair on the other side of the table. "Isn't that right, James?"

"News travels fast," he said, frowning.

"Don't blame me. It's your system that leaks, obviously."
I folded my arms, not sure why I was being defensive.
Maybe I still hadn't gotten my head around the whole thing.
I mean, how often did one get to know, albeit superficially, a
serial killer? It must be shock.

"Hey, Lily!" Imani came towards me, her white teeth
bright against her gorgeous dark skin as she grinned.

"Hey, Imani!" We hugged. I hadn't seen her for a couple
of weeks. She was an agent I'd met during the care-home
investigation and the latest addition to our snake-hunting
team. I'd introduced her to Liv, and we'd made plans to
have a girls' night out, but it hadn't yet eventuated. This was
her first time at one of our meetings, but I was pretty sure
she and Liv crossed paths at the PIB.

"Hey, Liv!" Imani gave her a hug too. Her enthusiasm
was contagious, and I was still smiling, despite the tension
hovering at the corner of my vision.

Will put his arm around me and squeezed. We sat next
to each other at the table, and I waved at Angelica, who sat
at the head, a couple of chairs to my left. "Hello, dear." She
didn't smile.

Angelica wasn't the smiliest of people, but she usually
greeted me with slightly more joy than that. "Hi."

"I'm sure I don't need to remind you not to talk to
anyone about the Frazer case, and that includes the media
and his family. You haven't said anything, have you?"

Sheesh, did she think I was stupid? I sighed. "Of course
not. I'm not an idiot."

"Someone's snappy tonight. What's up?" James knew I wasn't normally cranky, and maybe he was saying something so I didn't make it worse for myself. Crossing Angelica was never a good thing, not that I'd actually done anything terrible, but I'd only just started digging my hole. Given more time, who knew what I could achieve.

"I don't know. There's a lot going on. I'm probably still getting over the weekend. Marcia, the lady I was actually working for, is really nice. She's Jeremy's grandmother. I just hate that she's going through all this. She just turned eighty. And to be honest, Jeremy was really nice. I'm having trouble reconciling the fact that he's a nice person yet possibly a serial killer."

"Don't worry, Lily." Will put his arm around me and rubbed my arm. "Let us figure it out. Just be honest when you're called to the witness box, and let the evidence speak for itself. Whatever you have to say is not going to be the deciding factor on whether or not he goes to jail. Okay?"

I nodded. "Mm hmm."

"Okay, everyone, please take a seat. We need to move this meeting along. I do need to get some sleep before work tomorrow morning." Angelica's poker face was on, and her businesslike voice turned her into Ma'am before my eyes. She was always so dry, but her touch of humour didn't escape me. Blink and you'd miss it. "I'd like to start by welcoming Imani. We'll get you to swear in now, dear. As you know, your promise is binding."

Imani nodded. "Yes, Ma'am."

The golden book appeared in the air in front of her, the

room thrumming with power. She placed her hand on it and repeated the words Ma'am asked her to. When they were done, the book disappeared in a flash of light. "Good, now we can continue." Ma'am went over everything we knew so far. "And that brings us to Lily and Will's discovery."

Hmm, Lily and Will. We could start a homewares shop with that name combination. I liked it.

"Why are you smiling, Lily? What's so funny? Your reaction to this situation is alarming, to be honest. You've been acting strangely since you came in."

My head jerked towards Ma'am. Everyone was staring at me. My cheeks heated, and I felt thirteen again in a room full of judgemental adults. "Sorry, my mind wandered." Will snorted, so I elbowed him in the ribs. His grunt brought me much satisfaction. "Please continue. I promise not to smile again." Wow, what a miserable promise to make but, I had to admit, appropriate.

"Thank you. Now, as I was saying, the evidence they uncovered at lunch was enlightening, to say the least. Unfortunately, it's led to more questions, but it's filled in a potential link previously unknown to us between the disappearance of Lily's parents and Regula Pythonissam. That common link being Dana. The role her parents have to play in all this will be clearer by the end of this meeting."

Liv breathed a quiet, "Oh, wow." I, on the other hand, was a little more put out.

I looked at Will, my mouth agape. He gave me a quick nod, possibly indicating he knew what the information was. Why hadn't he told me earlier? It's not like he hadn't had time. I shut my mouth and jammed my back teeth together. More secrets between us? I was one unhappy witch. Grrr.

Liv gave me a sympathetic glance, as did Beren. James's gaze was fixed on the table. Maybe he was gathering his thoughts? I had no idea if he already knew what the information was, but talking about our parents was always difficult for both of us.

Ma'am continued. "So, what we've found out is that about a month before your parents went missing, Dana's mother died. Dana's father, who worked for us at the time, had a breakdown and left the PIB. He moved away, taking Dana with him. His address was listed as a property in Spain. He wasn't one of our top agents and didn't have security clearance on top-secret files, so after initially confirming he lived there, we didn't keep tabs on him. Recent enquiries reveal he no longer lives there. He still owns the place, but it's been rented as holiday accommodation for the past nine years."

So, that meant they'd only lived there for about a year. "Where did they go after that?"

"We can't find any new addresses. Dana surfaced when she was eighteen, a couple of years after her father quit, and started working for us. Her father may have been floating around, but there are no listed addresses for him for any time between the time he left and now."

"Do we know how her mother died?" Imani asked.

James and Angelica looked at each other. James answered, "No. All the records we held pertaining to Dana's father have disappeared, and the mother never worked for us. We had a brief dossier on her, but that's gone too. There are no medical records confirming what happened, or police reports. All we have is one newspaper clipping found at the local library with the news story of Dana's family home burning to the ground. The mother, according to the article, was said to have been inside. Bones were recovered by the authorities and confirmed as hers, but by normal human channels, not by the PIB. Her father had the bones cremated and took them with him."

Oh, could you cremate already burnt remains? I supposed witches could do whatever they wanted if their magic skills were up to it. But what a horrible way to die. That poor woman. "So you don't know whether her death was an accident or not?"

James shook his head. "No, and we have no way of finding out, except maybe…." He stared at me. Everyone stared at me, well, except Imani—she looked at everyone else, a confused expression on her face.

"Um, does Imani's oath cover knowing about my talent?" I trusted her, but things could change, and I didn't know her very well at all. Who was to say we wouldn't have an argument in the future and she wasn't the sort of person who would take what revenge she could, just for the fun of it?

Imani stood and came around to my side of the table. She placed a hand on my shoulder. Power warmed the spot and spread through my body. "I, Imani Jawara, swear that I will not divulge any information about Lily's talents to anyone who does not already know. If I do, may my magic and talent be given freely and in its entirety to Lily Bianchi, for her to do with as she pleases. I swear to protect Lily with my life as long as I am able."

Fiery heat scorched my shoulder where her palm rested. We both cried, "Ow!" and then it was done. The pain disappeared, and she slid her hand off. We stared at each other. What the hell had just happened? And why, oh why, had she sworn to protect my life with her own? This was crazy.

Silence lingered, heavier than the aftermath of a politically incorrect joke. Divots marred the space between Ma'am's brows, and James's stern expression made him look older than his twenty-eight years. They watched Imani, assessing. I looked up at her, my shoulder itching. "Why?" My befuddled brain only transmitted one word for me, but there wasn't much else to convey. She was sure to know what I was really asking.

Her sassy, lyrical accent was sober yet unapologetic. "I wasn't initially going to do that, but when I touched you, it became clear. You're the one, Lily. I've told you that before. Without you, the world as we know it is going to change to a dark and soulless place. I can't let that happen. Just swearing my allegiance to you has made me feel lighter somehow. It was the right thing to do." She smiled and nodded. "No regrets."

"Um, well, thank you. I need time to digest all this, but you've earned the right to know my secret talent. I can see the past through my camera. I can also see when someone is going to die." I swallowed the stupid lump that always preceded my tears. "That's how I knew something terrible was going to happen at the care home. I knew Beren and Ma'am were going to die. And on Saturday, I took a picture that showed a long-dead body that wasn't actually there. It turned out to be one of the murdered women Jeremy's been accused of killing."

"How do you know that?" James asked.

"Well, I don't *know*, know. I figured. I knew three women had been killed in a similar way because I spoke to you about it all. Remember? It can't be a coincidence that Jeremy's been charged with three additional murders. And they said the newest body was found with unusual wounds, but they wouldn't say what. So, yes, I'm making assumptions, but considering I took that photo at the back of his gran's property, can you blame me? Not to mention, you were trying to link him to those murders ever since I sent you that photo."

He pressed his lips together but said nothing. Ma'am slapped the table. Everyone jumped, and my heart made a break for the outside. I held my hand over it and pressed down. *You're staying there for now. Don't get any ideas.* It made me think of the dead women with the missing hearts. I shuddered.

Ma'am's gaze rested on James, then me, the weight of her displeasure palpable. "We'll discuss this later. We're not here to talk about a case that you're no longer involved in, Lily. Now, Imani—" Her attention turned to the agent, and I let out a large breath. The relief was not dissimilar to almost dropping your phone on concrete but catching it at the last moment, or actually dropping it face down and picking it up to find it was unscathed. Time to buy a lottery ticket. Or had my good luck all been used up now?

Ma'am continued. "We'll discuss what you just did later, in private. For now, get back to your seat."

Imani met Ma'am's stare with an unrepentant stare of her own. Well, if I was going to have someone swear to protect me with their life, it may as well be someone who would face anything or anyone, which she clearly would. She was the only person I knew—other than stupid Dana—who wasn't related to Angelica but who had nerves of titanium and could stand up to her. Even if I or Beren or even James stood up to her—which was super rare—we always softened a bit at the end, apologised, or at least *looked* sorry. There was nothing apologetic about Imani's strut or the way she sat back at the table, confidently, back straight but face relaxed. Girl had game.

Ma'am cleared her throat. A glass of water appeared in her hand, and she took a sip, then continued. "Lily, therefore, can go to the property and take some photos. The current owners built a new house about five years ago. They're not witches. I'm sure a simple no-notice spell will suffice."

Trespassing wasn't something I felt great about, but we needed to find more clues. My parents' disappearance may have had nothing to do with Dana's mother's death, but maybe it had everything to do with it. We wouldn't know till we followed all our leads. "Does the new house sit on the same spot as the old one?"

"Does it matter?" asked Beren.

"Yes. I need to be in a spot where I could have seen something if I'd been there when it was happening. If the new house is there, we'll have to break in for me to actually see anything. Look, even if I can't get inside, there's a chance I'll still find some clues. Maybe whoever burnt the house down was outside at some point before or during the fire?" Hmm, but if they were witches, they'd normally use the reception room. Damn.

"Can you go tomorrow night?" Angelica asked.

"Ah. Um." My brain scrambled to keep up. That was unexpected. I didn't want to sneak around someone's property. "Are there any times no-notice spells don't really work?"

Angelica pursed her lips. "Yes, dear. If you make enough noise to attract attention, or if you touch the person. It will be dark. The family who lives there will be inside their house unaware of anything happening outside."

"Do they have a dog? What if there's a dog outside. Do those spells work on animals?"

James and Angelica shared a look. What it meant was beyond me, but the fact they had to share a silent message meant that maybe animals were immune. "Well?" I folded my arms.

Ma'am composed her poker face. "Yes, dear. Animals are immune to the spell." At least James had the decency to look guilty.

"Well, thanks. You could have at least warned me. I mean, shouldn't we have a plan to deal with the dog?"

"Stop fussing, dear. You're jumping to conclusions. You don't even know if they have a dog."

"Do you know? I mean, don't you check out everything before sending your agents into the field?" Will touched my arm, jammed his way between my folded arms, and pried them apart to hold my hand. Okay, so maybe I needed calming down. I didn't normally get so worked up, and I didn't know why I was, but could anyone really blame me?

"Lily." A warning note rang in James's tone. "Yes, there is a dog, okay. But Beren will be with you, and he will put him to sleep."

My eyes widened. "You're going to kill the dog?! You can't. That poor dog. What's wrong with you PIB people?"

James's brow wrinkled; then he laughed. "You idiot, Lily. He'll put him to *sleep*, as in, sleep for an hour and wake up again. Do you even know me, your own brother? You know I'd never condone something like that, let alone speak so calmly about it. What's gotten into you?"

"I don't know. Sorry. I've been on edge the past few days. I'll simmer down now." I relaxed my jaw, and Will squeezed my hand, then caressed it with his thumb. Warm comfort seeped into me. I gave him a small smile, grateful for his support. Being this stressed was tiring. Why was I feeling like this? I needed to get a grip. I much preferred myself easygoing and happy.

Angelica took another sip of water and disappeared the glass with a wave. "Now we have that sorted, I'll confirm that you and Beren will meet at my place tomorrow at 9:00 pm.

You can travel from there to a one-use spot across the road amidst the trees that Beren will set during the day tomorrow. If there are any issues with the dog, or otherwise, I want you to just pop out of there straight away, and it won't do to have one of our cars somewhere it can be seen." I didn't know much about one-use spots. Normally we witches could only travel to a properly designated spot we knew the coordinates for. Of course, they were private spots—like a toilet cubicle —so that we were never spied by an unsuspecting human.

"One-use spots sound so convenient. Why don't we use them more?" Well, if I didn't ask, I would never find out. Ma'am was supposed to be my witch mentor, but she was always short on time and hardly ever volunteered information. I had to work for everything.

"One-use spots are fickle, dear. If you set one to use later and another witch happens to go somewhere nearby, they might end up in your spot, and when you need to use it, it won't be there. Or, you could accidentally end up being sucked into someone else's nearby spot. And of course, there is always the risk someone will see you. We don't encourage using them. Permanently set ones are much more reliable and safer."

"Oh. Okay." I should look into what made them less stable. Sounded like an accuracy problem and a discoverability thing. What if you could make it so it would reject anyone who wasn't you? Hmm, something to think about... like I needed more crap to occupy my brain. Being me was tiring.

Ma'am nodded at James. "Please report on the two agents we've been watching."

James gave a nod. "Yes, Ma'am. Agents Price and Bard." James flicked his hand, and two sheets of A4 paper appeared in front of each person. Each sheet had a photo of one agent and basic information: height, age, weight, address, witch talent, years working for the PIB. Agent Price was twenty-eight, dusky brown skin, shaved head, huge muscles, and six foot tall. Agent Bard was thirty, pale-skinned, and thin with lanky arms and legs for his five-foot-eleven frame, which wasn't the usual build. Agents normally worked out a lot and had some kind of muscled bod happening, but since lots of what they did was with magic, they probably didn't need to be super fit. Maybe some of them just wanted to look more intimidating, but then again, some criminals and situations were violent and were more easily handled by strong guys.

James continued. "They only became Facebook friends two years ago. Prior to that, they don't appear to have had contact with each other outside the PIB, and they rarely work together. In fact, they've only partnered up on a case once since Price joined us five years ago. Observing them at work, they stay away from each other and only give a brief nod when passing each other in the cafeteria or hallways. On Facebook, they chat all the time, comment on each other's posts, and there's a couple of pictures showing them out together."

That was weird. "If they want to pretend they don't

know each other, isn't Facebook a dead giveaway?" How good were these agents, really?

"Good question, Lily. They go by nicknames on Facebook: Rob Pricey and Shakespeare Smith. We found them by using facial recognition software. Although a spell would have done the trick too, we don't want to alert anyone to our surveillance, and a spell might have tripped an alarm on their end. We have no idea how sophisticated their witchy technological skills are. We've had to keep physical surveillance at a minimum—they're trained agents, and they would notice that in an instant."

"Other than Agent Price's tattoo, have we linked them in any way to Regula Pythonissam?" Will asked.

James regarded Will for a beat too long before he said, "No, but we're working on it. We have to send someone undercover to infiltrate their little twosome with a view to becoming a member of the group."

Something struck me. "Will, did Dana ever try and rope you into joining the group? I mean, she wouldn't have come out and said it, but do you remember anything unusual that she took you to or asked you about? Because, honestly, if she could trust anyone, it was the man who... loved her." Damn, some words were hard to say. Yes, their relationship was in the past, but the fact that he'd loved her still grated on me. Deep down, maybe she still owned a piece of him. *Gah, not now, brain. Stop.*

He stared at the far wall, probably thinking. "Like I told you before, Lily, she never wanted me to meet her parents, but I never knew her mother was dead—she kept that information to herself. As for joining groups, we went out with her friends a few times—friends she said she went to school with, but, come to think of it, they never mentioned anything to do with their school years." His brow wrinkled. "Whenever I asked a question about their school years, someone always interrupted with 'let's do a shot' or with some irrelevant story about something different. I only ever asked a handful of times, and I never thought it was strange until right now."

I shrugged. "Well, you didn't have any reason to be suspicious. You trusted her, took her at her word."

"True, but I'm an agent, Lily. My feelings for someone shouldn't dampen my instincts. I did think it odd that two of her school friends were five years older than her, but I figured she was just popular and must have known their younger siblings or something."

Ma'am rubbed her chin. "Will, were there any times you were suspicious of where she went? Did you ever feel that she wasn't telling you everything?"

"Not really. After the whole tea incident, I took some time to think back to when we were together, see if there was anything I'd missed that looked suspicious in hindsight. There were a few times she'd just up and leave for two or three days with the excuse it was a friend emergency, or a girls' weekend. She usually had them organised for when I was working. I briefly thought she might be having an affair, but then I remembered how awesome I was, and I thought, nah."

I raised a brow and laughed. "You're kidding, right? Please tell me you're kidding."

He grinned. "Of course I am. I did think she might be having an affair, but she was so attentive when she was with me, I really did discount it as unfounded jealousy, and I didn't think about it again. And look, it still might be nothing—she may have been hanging out with her friends, but… maybe not. In any case, it will be virtually impossible to figure out where she was and what she was doing. What we could do is some background checks on those friends of hers. They're probably still around. I don't have their addresses, but I remember their names, and I even have the phone number for her closest girlfriend, Anna. They supposedly went to the same school since they were in second year."

Millicent made some notes. "Okay, I'll get on that tomorrow. Just write down that info now and give it to me. I'm trying to avoid anything electronic, especially from your phone, just in case she's managed to find a way around our blocking spells."

"Fair enough." Will conjured a piece of paper and a pen and got writing, then handed it to Millicent.

Ma'am glanced at me before focussing on Will. My spidey senses were going off. What was that look about? There was a high chance I wasn't going to like what was about to unfold. "Will, dear, I have a favour to ask." Well, this was highly unusual—Ma'am asking rather than demanding. I held my breath, waiting for her to drop the bomb. It wasn't a matter of *if* there would be carnage, just how much. "We need more information. I'm going to put you on a case with Bard. I'd like you to get friendly with him, but make it subtle. When you have his trust, I'd like you to play up the missing Dana angle. I want him to think you still love her and you're torn between that and the fact that she's a criminal."

Will stared at Ma'am, his serious look not giving too much away. He turned to me, his gaze softening. "Are you okay with this?"

I nodded. "It's not like you'll be dating Piranha again, so yeah, of course it's okay." I ignored the worms of discomfort in my stomach. It was scary that he would be made to confront his feelings for her, but I sensed that wouldn't be the worst of it. He turned back to Ma'am. "I'll do it."

She smiled. "Good. I have an investigation starting tomorrow that I'll get you both on. Meeting's at ten. Be there. Tomorrow, I'd like for you and Lily to go for a run in the morning. During that run, in a very public place, I want you to have an argument and break up."

My mouth dropped open. What the actual—

"What?" At least Will was on the same page.

"For sure Dana is spying on you and Lily—Lily is her ultimate prize, after all. I'm sure anything that hurts Lily will make Dana very happy. We need her to lower her guard, maybe eventually try and make contact with you again. If she thinks she has an in, I'm sure she'll go for you, if for no other reason than to hurt Lily."

And there it was. Boom! Blood and guts everywhere. My stomach was under my chair, and my heart splatted on the wall. There it went, sliding down, leaving a smeary mess before resting on the floor. Total carnage. "Well, there goes our weekend at your place."

He looked into my eyes, the pain in his evident. "Sorry, Lily. But we need to do this. You know that, right?"

I sighed. "Yeah, yeah. Whatever." Sadness swept over me. "At least it's only pretend. How long will we have to do this for?"

"Will's assignment is estimated to last a couple of weeks, and we'll likely need more time. How long is a piece of string? It depends on how quickly the information gets relayed to Dana and how long she takes to respond. We'll be monitoring the situation closely, though, so if we can get a read on where she is before she responds, we can move on to the next stage, which is finding out who the other members are, where they are, and what their objective is. Because your parents going missing was just the beginning, Lily. There's no use us giving ourselves away when there's so much left to discover. Right now, our advantage is that they don't know your talent, and they don't realise we even know of their group. We need to play that as far as possible."

"Yes, Ma'am." This hurt like hell, but the temptation to find out more about Regula Pythonissam and what happened to my parents was too strong to ignore. That's what we were here for, and no one had ever said it was going to be easy. I was here to fight and fight hard, no matter what it cost.

I took his hand and squeezed. "What time do you want to run?"

He squeezed it back. "I'll be there at seven." We stared into each other's eyes until someone cleared their throat—whether it was Ma'am or James, I couldn't tell.

Ma'am addressed Imani. "I have a job for you, Imani. I'd like you to go through these and see if you can use your talent to pick out relevant entries." My mum's diaries appeared on the table in front of Imani. "Rather than Lily wasting time running all over the countryside, I'd like to see if we can pinpoint only the important events. Once that's done, you can accompany her to photograph them. I'll feel better knowing she's protected. James and Beren will be too busy working cases, and Will is off limits to her, so that leaves you, and since you've sworn to protect her with your life…."

"Yes, Ma'am. It would be my pleasure." Imani turned to me and smiled. She radiated peace and niceness, and I had to smile back, even if the meeting had been rather heavy. "I might also have more visions or feelings about what's going on. The more time I spend with Lily, the more I'll pick up on."

"Good. You have a short two-day assignment coming up, but after that, I'll give you a day off to go through those diaries and see what you can find. We'll discuss it here in a week—I don't want to overload our group and spread ourselves too thin. For now, we have as much as we can handle. This is a marathon, not a sprint. Remember that, people. Any questions?" She folded her hands on the table, her poker face erring on the side of relaxed. Easy for some. "No? Good. Same time next week. And Beren can relay any information you find at the property tonight. I'll get Milli-cent and Olivia to follow up during the week." She stood. "Good night, all. And good luck tomorrow, Lily and Will."

She stepped away from the table and disappeared. Olivia put her arm around me and leaned down. "Wow, tough break. Are you okay?"

"Yeah. I'll be fine. I don't have a choice, and I won't let this become more than it should. We need to do this, and I trust Will." I looked at him and smiled.

He leaned down and kissed my forehead. "The time will go faster than you think. We'll just have to postpone our sleepover, but I'll be thinking about it… a lot." He grinned.

A swell of affection and happiness filled my heart. I returned his grin. "Maybe we need to go home now and say a proper goodbye." I waggled my eyebrows. His eyes widened. "Well, not that proper. Or… more proper than improper?" I laughed and blushed. I hadn't been suggesting sex, for goodness' sake.

Olivia snorted. "Go for improper, I say." She lifted her gaze to watch Beren, who was talking to James and Imani.

"You'll probably get there before I will."

"I hope so."

Will and I looked at each other and laughed. "Why are we laughing?" I asked. "That's actually so sad. To be honest, I'm sick of waiting, but yeah, tonight isn't the right time."

"No, but you're not getting away with just a kiss on the cheek, missy. Let's go."

"Ooh, a take-charge guy. Nice." I turned to Olivia. "Are you coming?"

"Hang on." She called across the table to Beren. "Hey, B, can you give me a lift home later?"

He smiled. "Can I ever. I'll be ready in five."

Olivia turned back to me, her head held high. She waved her arm in a regal dismissal. "You may go."

"Ha ha. Thanks, oh Queen. I'll see you later."

Will grabbed my hand, and as we stepped through the doorway, my butterflies took flight. *Smoochy goodbye, here I come.*

CHAPTER 10

Argh. Six thirty was way too early to be getting up. It was pitch-black outside and would be for at least another hour. The trees outside my window stirred in the sprinkling rain and light breeze. It was going to be f-f-f-freezing out there. I checked the weather on my phone. Starting at five Celsius, rising to a whopping ten! Great.

I magicked on long tights, sports bra, long-sleeve tee, and a jacket I could unzip and tie around my waist. The house was quiet and dark as I made my way downstairs. Olivia wouldn't start work until eight, so she'd get to sleep for another forty-five minutes. Lucky duck. Hmm, or was I the duck, going out in the rain when inside was so much nicer?

As I sipped my coffee at the kitchen table, I decided to treat myself when I got home. I'd light the fire in the living room and take a couple of hours to just read and relax—goodness knew I'd had no decompression time lately. And later I'd edit poor Marcia's photos. At least she'd have some nice memories of her birthday. Saying goodbye to Will this morning for the last time in who knew how long was going to suck, but that didn't mean the rest of my day had to. Maybe I'd even grab a takeaway double-chocolate muffin and cappuccino to bring back and enjoy by the fire. I smiled.

Coffee finished, I looked at my phone. Five minutes until Will was supposed to arrive. Restless, I stood and stretched my legs. It was cold out, and I didn't want an injury. Just as I finished my quads, there was a light tap on the reception-room door. I grinned and ran to open it.

Sexy in black, he stepped through the door and caught me in his embrace. I inhaled the fresh scent of his deodorant and tipped my head up for a kiss. Okay, so getting up early wasn't all bad when this was the reward. When we were done, he cleared his throat and grinned. "That's the best pre-run hello I've ever had."

"I'm awesome like that." I smirked.

"Mmm, you definitely are." He sighed. "But now we have to go out in the rain and do our duty. Are you ready?"

"No." I frowned. "Can we at least get fifteen minutes in before we fight. I really need the exercise."

He shook his head. "You're a weirdo, but okay."

"How is wanting my exercise weird? It sets me up for the day and means I can eat the double-chocolate muffin without feeling guilty for the rest of the week."

"Can't you just eat what you want? I can."

I rolled my eyes. Typical man—he had no idea what it took for us ladies to keep control of our fat cells. I had way more to corral than he had, and they were stubborn—they refused to stop asking for food, and they didn't want to be shrinking violets, hidden away where no one could see. Each one tried to be bigger than the rest, practically jumping up and down saying, "Look at me. Look at me!" Life so wasn't fair sometimes. "Yeah, yeah, show off. Let's go."

As soon as I opened the front door, the cold air slapped me, one-two, on both cheeks. Greeting the day was a violent affair some mornings. Wanting to warm up quickly, I set off at a good pace, Will hurrying to catch up. We got into a rhythm, jogging next to each other, the only sound our puffing breaths, muffled footfalls, and the occasional car driving past. There was serenity to the fog swimming across the fields we passed, to the other walkers quietly starting their day, with or without their dogs.

Unfortunately, we were about to shatter the calm.

We were approaching a bus stop where a few people, rugged up in coats and huddled under umbrellas, waited for their bus to work. There were plenty of places a person spying could watch from—behind parked vehicles, in gardens behind fences, or maybe they were following us with some kind of invisible, silent witchy drone—as far as I knew, there was no such thing, but hey, anything was possible, and I still didn't know half of what existed for witches. Now was as good a time as any to fake the end of our relationship.

I puffed out, "Hey, what time do you want me to come over this weekend?" We had to start somewhere. I had no idea how this was going to play out, but I would pretend it was my reality so it looked real. Any doubts anyone had about our separation would make this a waste of time and endanger Will when he enacted the second part to this—infiltrating her friend network.

"Ah, about that." He stopped just past the bus stop, within hearing distance of the commuters. I stopped next to him and jogged on the spot. "I've been thinking about it, and, well…."

I furrowed my brow. "What do you mean by well?"

He put his hands on his hips and looked at me warily. "I can't do this anymore. I need some space. I'm sorry, Lily."

My feet slowed to a stop. "What?" I let the reality of it seep through me, drenching me like the rain had. Believing it was the key to giving a great performance. My stomach sunk to freeze in a puddle at my feet.

His eyes screamed sorry as he said the words I never wanted to hear. "I need a break. I don't want to see you anymore. I'm sorry. I really am." His sad voice, the regret in his gaze—well, it pulled a thread that kept unravelling. Tears scalded my eyes. He reached out to touch my shoulder. I stepped away.

"Don't touch me. How can you do this? Why? Is there someone else?" I all but cried.

He stared at me and blinked, the pause confirmation to our audience that there was, indeed, someone else. "I—I thought I could get over Dana, but I can't. I still love her, and I can't pretend anymore. Shit." He turned around, then turned back to face me and ran a hand through his thick dark hair. He shook his head. "Please don't hate me. I'm sorry. I just can't. It's over for us, Lily. Sorry."

My tears spilled over as I let the horror flow through me, more uncomfortable than the freezing rain.

His eyes glistened—was he crying? He shook his head again, turned, and ran, like literally ran. His speed would have been impressive in any other scenario. I heard a lady behind me at the bus stop say, "Oh, no. That poor girl." And now, my shame would be complete because I was not running in the same direction as Will. I had to turn and go back past the commuters.

As I turned, the bus pulled up—thanks be to the gods. An older man and middle-aged woman gave me sympathetic looks replete with side head tilts as I jogged past. I gave a small nod in thanks and kept running. I sure hoped someone from Dana's crew had been watching and would report to her. It would totally suck if I'd just gone through that for nothing. It felt like a real break-up, and while I ran home, I kept wondering if there had been any truth to Will's words. *Gah, don't go there, Lily. He cares about you, and he doesn't love Dana.* But it wasn't time to convince myself, and, now that I thought about it, I was going to have to pretend to be miserable for the next who knew how many weeks. Oh my God! What if it turned into months? We really could be over by then. Long-distance relationships were difficult, but at least the participants could still talk to each other and even see each other on video calls, but Will and I had nothing. No contact allowed. Hmm, how were the weekly meetings about the snake group going to happen if we couldn't be seen together? Admittedly no one should know we were both going there, but what if Dana had figured out how to track both of us?

Damn. How had I not realised this before? Well, at least my miserableness wouldn't be pretend. I'd be able to pull that off with ease. Just great. On the way back, I continued past Angelica's and up to High Street to Costa. I grabbed my double-choc muffin and cappuccino and walked home —I didn't want to spill the coffee, of course. It was in a take-away cup, but coffee might still spurt out of the little hole at the top, and every drop was precious. I didn't want to waste any of it. It was all I had now, after all. No more Will, just coffee. Lots and lots and lots of coffee. Woe is me. I almost smiled because of my pity party, but then I remembered I shouldn't be smiling where anyone could see me, especially not this soon after my break up.

When I got home, I showered, then dressed in comfy tracky dacks—which was Aussie speak for tracksuit pants—and a soft long-sleeve T-shirt. I magicked the fire on, grabbed my breakfast and iPad and settled in for part two of my plan—relax for a couple of hours with a fun cosy mystery.

But then my phone rang, blowing my plan to hell. With the love-hate thing the universe and I had going on, how had I expected anything different?

CHAPTER 11

I picked my phone up and looked at the screen. It was a local number I didn't recognise. I wasn't prone to answering the phone unless I knew who was calling, but considering everything going on at the moment with the snake group, it might be important. "Hello?"

A tentative male voice said, "Lily?"

I scrunched my face. It was a familiar voice, but the owner of it didn't come to mind straight away. "Yes? Who's this?"

"It's Jeremy... you know, the famous guy who's been falsely accused of murder. I'm sorry to bother you, but I need your help. Please don't say no."

Um, wow. Did not see that coming. I wasn't sure why or how, but I might as well ask. "What did you need?" Maybe he just wanted a visitor to while away the torturous time in jail. Goodness knew I'd been there, and it was not fun. "I could get you some air freshener."

"What?"

"Um, never mind." Being a man, maybe he was used to stinky toilets, but having them in your bedroom-cum-living-area was not my idea of pleasant. Having been incarcerated a few months ago had scarred me for life. "So, what can I help with?"

"My solicitor sent me a letter. She's reneged on taking the case, and when I tried to get in touch with her, her receptionist said she's left town, but she wouldn't say why. I don't know what to do. And when my mother found out, she hired another lawyer without consulting me, and he's hopeless. If he takes my case, I'm going to jail for sure."

Had his solicitor figured he was guilty and dumped him? An ethical solicitor, hmm. Yeah, nah. It still didn't make sense to take a case and within a couple of days drop it. But then again, people were weird. Maybe she'd had a family emergency? "But what can I do? I'm not a solicitor."

"Word around here is that you're good at gathering evidence, that if it wasn't for you, a lot of crimes would have gone unsolved lately. There are a couple of crims in here who really hate you, Lily. But I've met a couple of nice guards, and they say the same thing: you're a bit of a legend around here."

Huh? Me, a legend. No way. I massaged my temples. Maybe that's why stupid Dana hated me. Maybe she didn't care one fig that Will might have liked me. She was always bragging about how she was better than me, after all.

Anyway, that was irrelevant right now. I wasn't sure about how I felt knowing I had any kind of reputation in that place, although I was sure I wasn't happy about crims having it in for me, but then, what did I expect?

"Lily? Are you still on the line?"

"Ah, yeah. Sorry, just thinking."

"You're my only hope. I know you don't owe me anything, and we hardly know each other, but I have a feeling that out of anyone I should call, it's you. I didn't do it. I could never kill anyone. If there's any doubt in your mind that I did it, help me, because that means the real murderer's out there right now, and who knows who'll be next. Please?" That please sounded like he was about to cry —a desperate man begging. I had to admit, if he was guilty and knew I was good at solving crimes, it was crazy for him to call me. If I was as good as he claimed I was, surely I'd be the last nail in his sentencing coffin? "I'll pay you what I was paying my lawyer."

I shook my head. "It's not about the money. I'm just not sure what you think I can do."

"Evidence, Lily. I need irrefutable evidence showing I didn't do it. Maybe you could even figure out who really did. The clown my mother got for me has no idea. Even he thinks I did it."

"Oh my God! Did he actually say that?"

"No, but I can tell. He looks at me like he thinks I did it, especially when he thinks I'm not watching, and when he smiles at me, it's fake as all get out. He'd make a terrible actor."

"Why can't you just fire him and get someone else?"

"There aren't too many witch lawyers around, Lily. We're dealing with the PIB. I tried a couple in London, but they didn't get back to me. I don't know why, but it feels like I've been black banned. Maybe everyone thinks I'm guilty?"

But I don't, not really. Oh. There was my answer. My gut feeling. I supposed that was the doubt he was talking about, and if I had even a smidgeon of it, I needed to find out who did it—for everyone's sakes. "Okay. I'll help. And I don't want your money."

He let out a large whoosh of air. "Thank you, Lily. Thank you, thank you, thank you! You don't know how much this means. And I'm still going to pay you."

"Look, we can argue about it later. The only thing I will say is that I may not be able to share all my... proof with you. If I do find anything, I'll need to figure out what hard evidence we can actually gather. What I do is more like getting hints of the truth, but then I have to dig the rest of the way for it."

"Ah... okay. But you can still figure it out, though, can't you?"

"I'll give it a damn good try, Jeremy. I do have a few questions to ask you. Maybe I should come see you?"

"That would be great. You have no idea how relieved I am. If you want to make an appointment to meet with me, they'll arrange a specially warded meeting room. You just need to call and speak to the Manager of Interviews PIB Incarceration Division. Have you got a pen and paper, and I'll give you the number?"

"I'll just put it in my phone. Hang on." I put my phone on speaker and brought up Notes. "Okay, shoot." He gave me the number, we said our goodbyes, and I sat there, kind of stunned, really. What the hell just happened? Would Angelica be upset that I was getting involved? She hadn't seemed too pleased with James and I discussing it last night. Oh, and anything I found out, I wouldn't be able to give to the PIB. What if I found he was guilty, and he wouldn't let me share it with anyone else? Did client-lawyer privilege still exist if I wasn't a lawyer? Crap. What was I getting myself into?

Okay, breathe, Lily, breathe. They already had evidence against him, supposedly, and if he wasn't so desperate, he wouldn't have called me, so it was unlikely he'd get off unless I could discover new evidence. Right. So chances were that I wouldn't be in a predicament of having to find a way to get incriminating evidence to Angelica or James, and if it came to that, I'd figure how to make it happen. That sounded awful, but there was no way I'd let a guilty person get off if I could help it.

I magicked a pen and paper to myself and wrote down a list of questions to ask Jeremy. When I was done, I called the PIB and made an appointment to see him. They were fitting me in tomorrow morning at nine. Okay, so now all I had to worry about was tonight when I went with Beren to Dana's old house. My life truly was hellish when looking for clues to my parents' disappearance was only one of the crappy things going on. Although maybe I should look at Jeremy's case as a good distraction from my "break-up" with Will.

Even though it was fake, it was real in a way—we couldn't see each other, no matter how much we wanted to.

Let the torture begin.

DRESSED ALL IN BLACK, I SAT IN FRONT OF THE FIRE IN ONE armchair while Olivia sat in the other. She was keeping me company until Beren showed up. I nervously caressed the Nikon with my thumb.

"I can't believe you're going to be helping Jeremy. I mean, you're going to be hanging out with one of the most famous actors of our time."

"I wouldn't go that far, and it's not as if he's in everyone's good books at the moment. What if I get a bad name for helping him?" I didn't really think that would happen, but you never knew.

"You'll at least be a little bit famous when it's all said and done."

"I hope not. I'm going to keep this as low-key as possible."

Voices filtered in from the hallway; then Angelica and Beren walked in. "Hi, ladies." We both turned and smiled at Beren—Olivia's grin was way wider than mine, and I couldn't help the warm ball of satisfaction that rolled through my stomach. They weren't openly dating yet, but I was sure it wouldn't be long till they finally made it official. "Are you ready, Lily?" His smile faded—he knew what I went through when faced with seeing my parents.

I sighed. "Yes. As ready as I can be." I held up my camera. "Let's do this." I stood and went over to him.

Beren looked down at me. "If anything happens, just come straight back here. Okay?"

I nodded and shuffled from foot to foot, nervous energy thrumming through me. "Let's get this over with." I grabbed his hand.

"Good luck," said Angelica as we stepped through Beren's doorway.

We came out of the doorway, feet crunching on a bed of autumn leaves. The frigid air snapped at my skin, and I snuggled deeper into my coat. Beren looked around, likely getting his bearings. He whispered, "See those lights?" He pointed to two small elevated windows shining across the road about one hundred metres away. "That's where it is. When we get to the property line, use your talent to see where the house was originally. The less wandering around we do, the better."

"Ya think?"

"Snappy much?"

"You would be if you'd had the day I've had."

He put his hand on my back and rubbed up and down a few times. "I know. Sorry, Lily. Will told me what happened. Are you okay?" I wasn't sure if he just meant because we couldn't see each other or if he was keeping up the act in case we were being spied on, but if the snake group were spying on us right now, they'd surely figure out we were up to something to do with them, and that would start a whole new world of pain for all of us.

"I'll live." I created a bubble of silence. "You don't think they're listening, do you?"

"No. It would be impossible for them to track us while we travelled. But you can never be too careful. Okay, ditch that bubble, and let's get this done."

I did as he asked, and we crossed the quiet country lane. A fox howled in the distance. An owl hooted. I put the lens cap in my pocket and flicked my camera on as we jogged up the slight incline. The house was on a small rise behind a five-foot tall fence. The gate was open—lucky us, although I was sure a small amount of magic would've been enough to open it. The only risk would be if the homeowners were witches—we had no way of knowing. Witches didn't have to register with any witchy authorities at birth. Did the PIB actually know how many witches existed? Maybe they should have made it a thing to do, but how in the hell would you police something like that?

We stopped just before going through the gate. Beren was likely listening and watching for any dogs too. But if they'd had one roaming around, the gate probably would have been closed. Phew for us. I raised my camera and asked the universe to show me where the house had stood.

Night became day, and I shivered, feeling exposed in the sudden sunlight before reminding myself that it was still night-time in the real world. About ten metres to the right of the existing house was where Dana's house had stood—a two-storey timber barn conversion. A gorgeous home, it looked to be full of character yet newly renovated. Had it been a project for her parents? If so, they had good taste.

The slats were silvery grey. Large picture windows were evenly spaced, and it was capped off by a dark slate roof.

I lowered my camera and was swathed in darkness once again. Beren gave me a questioning look. "Over there," I whispered and pointed. With several glances towards the existing house to make sure we weren't discovered, we made our way to where the old house once stood. My photos wouldn't show up anything inside unless I was in there too. I hadn't worked out how to take photos through walls, even if they were walls that were no longer there. I grimaced. That didn't really make sense, but nothing about my life had since my twenty-fourth birthday, and I didn't know that it ever would again.

I looked through the viewfinder to orientate myself. I was standing about five metres in front of the building. May as well start here to make sure I didn't miss anything. "Show me the last time my parents were here." I held my breath. If my parents had only ever travelled there, this would show me nothing.

We were back to night-time, and I released my breath at what appeared through the lens. My parents' backs were to me as they stood at the front door, about to enter. Dana's mother held the door open. Welcoming, yellow-tinged light shone from behind her and spilled outside, casting shadows of my parents on the ground behind them. If I reached out a foot, I could almost touch their inky likenesses.

Dana's mother wore a huge smile, obviously happy to see my parents. Was this the night of the fire or a random get-together? Whatever it was, I had to assume it was important, or my magic probably wouldn't show anything. Or maybe it was just the only time they'd ever driven there rather than travelled.

I lowered my camera and showed Beren the pictures so he could see where we were. His eyes widened, and he shook his head. He blew out a breath. "No matter how many times I see these photos, I never get used to them." He looked up at the darkness in front of us, where there was nothing but stunted grass. "It's creeping me out tonight, to be honest." He rubbed one forearm as if banishing goosebumps.

"Tell me about it." I shivered. "And it's only going to get worse. I'm going to be asking some hard questions, B." If the universe showed me this house burning with people inside....

I took a deep breath and walked into what would have been the front vestibule. Looking through the lens again, I took in the vaulted ceiling and magnificent chandelier that lit the entry. Something was off, though. It was like I was viewing things from my knees. I panned around at the side table that held a vase and framed photo of Dana and her parents, which looked to come to my chest. I pointed the camera at my body. Ah, that's why! The house was no longer here, and since I was standing on the ground, I wasn't standing at floor level. Everything beneath my knees hid below the timber floor.

I clicked a couple of shots and showed Beren, who had stopped next to me. He nodded. Holding my camera up, I followed the image through a tall doorway and into a massive living area that was two-stories tall. Thick beams criss-crossed the span, pendant lights hanging from them, casting a warm glow over the whole area. On my left, huge three-metre tall windows started at the floor and ran in a row of four till they reached the open-plan kitchen. On the right, about halfway across on the second level, a walkway looked over the space. Bookshelves filled with books lined the walkway, and a door led to what was probably another corridor to bedrooms. This was one hell of an impressive home.

I snapped a couple of shots and again showed Beren. "Wow," he breathed. "Nice digs."

"Nice, indeed. What a shame it burnt down." I frowned. Even sadder was that someone had died. But why? I hoped we found out tonight. *Please, can my parents have had nothing to do with it.*

I didn't know if I was going to have to wander around for this next question, or even if I'd get the answer I wanted, but I needed to ask it nevertheless. "Show me where the fire started."

Dana's mother lay on one of their plush camel-coloured leather lounges only a couple of metres from where I stood. I clicked off several shots as I turned, taking in the whole room and the upstairs walkway. Standing in the kitchen, in front of another door, was Dana's father. He held his hand aloft. It was at the same height as the burning material that hovered over the couch his wife lay on. She must have been asleep when it happened. Magically induced sleep?

Dana's dad's face held regret, sadness, but not horrendous grief. And Dana's mum wasn't wearing the same dress she'd had on while greeting my parents at the front door. I guess we could narrow down when they would have been here based on their travel records to the UK. It would have been while I was alive—and judging by how they looked, not too long before they disappeared.

I turned back to the couch. Would the fire settle on Dana's mother first? Surely that would be too cruel and would have woken her up. I drew in a sharp breath. Oh. My. God.

Beren's voice sounded far away. "Lily, what's wrong?"

Nausea frothed the contents of my gut, slamming those bits of food against my stomach walls as if they were a boat in a storm, and heat just short of scalding slid uncomfortably from my hands up my arms. Sweat slicked my fingers and brow.

The fiery material flickered and sank towards the couch. I clicked the shutter button, photographing as it went, instinct kicking in because I sure as hell didn't have my wits about me in that moment. The flaming cloth landed on the cushion at Dana's mother's feet and set it alight.

The vision and warmth halted as if nothing had changed or moved. I snapped a few shots from different angles, my brain trying to comprehend what was going on. Was it a magical glitch, or was it because my witchy talent was getting stronger?

I pointed my camera towards Dana's father. His arm was by his side, his head bowed. So it definitely had been him. He didn't move, thank God. I shut my eyes and asked,

"Where did he get out?" When I opened my eyes, Dana's father was just gone. He must have magicked himself out. I went through the kitchen and found the back door, which was closed. I hurried to the front door, and tripped, twisting my ankle as I stepped into a small hole. "Ow!" Pain stabbed through my ankle and down to my heel. *Stupid, Lily. Stupid.* Without lowering my camera, I hobbled to the front door. It was shut.

Beren grabbed my arm. "Lily, are you all right? Look at me, please."

I lowered the camera and looked into his eyes. His brow wrinkled in concern—I seemed to have a habit of making people wrinkly. "I'm okay. I just…." I shook my head. Had it recorded on my camera as a video? I flicked my camera over to view the photos. There was no video. Would it work if I did have it as a video? Should I just have it on video the whole time even if it's just one photo since I'm walking around and getting all angles? That would make sense, and I didn't see why it wouldn't work. "Hang on. I just need to test something."

I switched it to record video. I didn't want to deal with anything stressful again tonight—I'd definitely had enough —so I just asked to see the house. I walked around the vestibule and out through the front door while I recorded. When I was done, I tried to play it back. It worked.

Beren watched over my shoulder. "Shit, Lily. You can video it instead of taking all the different angles separately. Did you know that before?"

"Obviously not or I would have done it." My voice was

devoid of bite, but I still felt bad. This was my buddy, B. He was one of the nicest people I knew. "Sorry. I didn't mean it like that. I'm just a bit shaken."

"From discovering you can video?"

"No." Bushes rustled near the existing house, and a dog barked. "Crap. I think it's time to get out of here. I'll see you back at Ma'am's."

With one last check over his shoulder, he whispered, "Last one back's a rotten egg."

Trust Beren to bring a smile to my face, despite what I'd just been through. I hastily made my doorway and stepped through... and straight into him.

"Ha ha, I beat you." He did a silly victory dance, arms waving all over the place.

"Yeah, yeah, but your dancing sucks."

"I'm saving the good stuff for the club. You just see my leftovers."

I laughed. "What kind of a friend are you? I'm taking back all the good words I put in for you to Liv." I smirked.

His smile dropped in faux horror. "You would not! Once spouted, they can't be unspouted. Anyway, she knows how awesome I am. She's beyond your influence in this." He winked.

"I can see the fear in your eyes. You know I'm her best friend, and she listens to everything I say. So you better watch it, buddy."

The door opened, and Angelica stood there, her brow raised. "Having fun, I see."

I shrugged. "Blowing off some steam. I just had a

crapola of a night. Come into the living room, and I'll explain why."

Angelica's eyes widened just enough to tell me she was surprised by my outburst. She glanced at Beren, who said, "You know almost as much as I do. But I don't think the news is all bad. She discovered something interesting."

"I did, but you don't know the full extent yet." I gently pushed past both of them and went through to the living area. "Liv!" I called, figuring she should be here for what I was about to reveal. Angelica could update everyone else later.

"Here I am," she yelled. Her stomping down the stairs echoed through to the living room. I sat on the Chesterfield closest to the window, facing the door. Beren sat next to me. Angelica and Liv sat opposite on the other Chesterfield. I handed my camera over and created a bubble of silence. "Have a look at the photos first. Then I'll tell you what else happened."

Liv looked at me. "Did someone see you?"

"No. Nothing like that. It's my talent."

Liv leaned over and looked at the photos as Angelica scrolled through. Angelica kept her poker face the entire time, but Liv's eyebrows rose, and her mouth dropped open, depending on what was on the screen. "So her father killed her mother?"

"That's inconclusive from the photos," said Beren. "She could have already been dead, and he just disposed of the body, but yes, he could have. Right now, obviously, he's the number one suspect."

"But could she have died of natural causes?" asked Liv.

Angelica had reached the end of the photos and was scrolling back. She stopped at the first picture of the flaming cloth, just before it started moving. "Would you burn someone in a house fire who had died of natural causes?" Angelica gave Liv a stern look.

Liv blushed. "Um, I guess not. I just… well, it could have been a weird witch thing." She shrugged.

"We're witches, not barbarians." Angelica's chin tipped into the air as she stared down at Liv.

"Sorry."

"That's okay, dear, but next time, think it through."

"Yes, Ma'am."

"Now that that's settled"—Angelica handed me my camera—"do you want to tell me about this series of photos?"

Of course she'd pick up on what was unusual. It gave me comfort that someone with her experience was on our side. But now it was time to spill. "While I was looking through the camera, the scene played like a movie. It wasn't for long, so maybe more like a GIF in length, but I watched it happening. I couldn't hear anything, and it made my hands so hot. Plus, I'm tired now, whereas before, I'd built my strength to the point that twenty minutes of using my talent wouldn't have made any difference." I yawned, unintentionally proving my point. Liv yawned, then Beren. I smiled. "Sorry." They both laughed.

"That's quite extraordinary, Lily." Angelica regarded me as one does a puzzle, but there was something else—a calculating gleam? She was probably trying to figure out when she could use my evolving talent to solve more crimes. As much as I loved justice and truth, I didn't want to spend my days filming the depraved doing evil stuff. What a terrible and depressing job. I took my hat off to law enforcement for having to deal with the scum of the earth every day, Angelica included, but it wasn't for me.

"Anyway, now what? How do we figure out if he killed her? And if it wasn't her, who was it, and why would he want to cover it up?"

Beren looked at his aunt. "Could he be protecting Dana?"

She pursed her lips. "It's possible."

Piranha was evil, but was she really that evil? "Will said she didn't talk to her parents. He didn't even know her mother had died. Maybe she killed her mother and couldn't face her father? Or maybe she was scared of what he might do if she showed up?"

"There are many questions that need answers. Right now, though, I'm going to have a cup of tea and read a book. I think a good night's sleep is in order, and I'll come up with a plan for our next meeting. We may be discovering this now, but it happened many years ago, Lily, and it won't be solved in five minutes. We're already understaffed at the bureau—I can't afford to waste anyone's time, so I'm going to plan first. We'll start by going down the most obvious route. When I decide what that is, I'll let you all know."

"Ah, okay." Was I disappointed? Hmm, yes. Yes, I was. I wanted to find out what happened to my parents, and I had a feeling this was connected in some way. Not to mention that if Dana had killed her mother, that made her one sick witch. There was no way she'd think twice about offing me, which made me wonder why she hadn't done it already—it was clear she hated me.

Someone else must want me alive.

But who?

CHAPTER 12

I sat across from Jeremy, at a stainless-steel table that was bolted to the floor. I guessed they didn't trust the inmates not to conk someone over the head with it in a bid to escape, or maybe in a fit of rage. The sterile surroundings took me back to when I'd been incarcerated for my brother's disappearance. As if I'd had anything to do with it or covering it up. I rolled my eyes. The PIB really did have a crappy track record, at least since I'd arrived. They either arrested the wrong people or employed people who were the opposite of what they needed.

Jeremy reminded me of how I'd felt when I'd been here —defeated and dishevelled. His hair looked as if he'd only been allowed to run his hand through it, and the bit on his crown stuck up—no hair stylists this side of the law. He had dark circles under his eyes and stubble, although the stubble did make him look a bit sexier. Hmm, I did not just think that. Nope. Okay, so I was human. I was pretty sure that Will perved on other women. It was reality, but he never flirted or strayed, at least, not that I'd noticed. Anyway, back to why I was here….

"Please help me, Lily. I thought I had a chance when I had the best solicitor going around, but she's disappeared. She still hasn't called me back to tell me why she reneged on taking my case. You said yes over the phone. Don't change your mind now." He sighed.

"But why me?" My stomach tensed as I waited for his answer. What if people had heard about my talent? I'd be in huge trouble. Whoever was after me would want me even more, along with every other idiot who wanted that power for themselves.

"Like I said before: the talk around here is that you're good at solving crimes. You've got a knack. Is that like your talent or something?"

"Um, not really. Kind of. I don't know. I do have *luck*, if you want to call it that. I seem to be able to stumble upon evidence sometimes, and I'm good at reading people." Okay, that last bit was a slight lie. I was sometimes good at reading people, but I had to tell him something so he wouldn't ask any more questions about my talent.

"Well, that's better than what I have now." He reached across the table with his magically-cuffed-together wrists and grabbed my hand in both of his. "Please. I didn't do this. I know it looks like it, but after Trudie left the other night, I stayed at Gran's. I didn't chase her down and kill her. I didn't even know where she went, and she didn't try to contact me again. As for those other women… I loved one of them. When she died, I was heartbroken. Everyone loved her. She was a gorgeous person, both inside and out. Gran still has our picture at her place." His smile was sad. He gently squeezed my hand and gazed into my eyes, his eyebrows drawn together. "Do you believe me?"

I squeezed back because the man in front of me was hurting big time. "I believe you, Jeremy, but I'll admit that you do look guilty."

"I have no motive for killing Amanda. I loved her, for goodness' sake."

"But the papers said you only briefly dated." Okay, so I hadn't read it in the papers, but I couldn't tell him I'd had a meeting with Angelica and James about this.

He released my hand and slid his back across the table and settled them on his lap. "I lied." He looked at his hands. "We'd been dating for six months, but I didn't want the public to know when we started dating, so if anyone asked, we'd say we were just friends. The usual. You know how it is." He looked back up and met my gaze.

"No, actually, I don't. I'm not famous. No one cares who I'm dating." I took my notepad and pen out of my bag and prepared to write. "So, you'd been dating for six months when she was killed?"

"Yes."

"Had you had any fights just before her death?"

He opened his mouth to answer when the door burst open. I swivelled quickly to face it. A tubby man dressed in a black suit, white shirt, and red-and-blue striped tie strode in,

Jeremy's evil mother in tow. "Don't say another word, Jeremy. She"—he pointed at me, the finger at the end of his outstretched arm stopping an inch from my nose—"works for the enemy."

I leant my head back and went a little cross-eyed. I batted his hand out of the way. "Watch where you put that thing." I folded my arms and looked up at him while ignoring Jeremy's mother. As much as I didn't want to see her, the room was small, and her glare was hard to miss, seeing as how she was looking over Mr Tubby's shoulder.

"What?" asked Jeremy.

"Your girlfriend here," said his mother. "She lives with the head of the PIB. Her brother's an agent too."

Jeremy turned questioning eyes my way. "Is this true, Lily?"

"Well, Angelica isn't the *head*, head. She's kind of like the managing director, but yes, I live with her, and my brother's an agent. But I'm not working for them. They don't even know I'm here."

He nodded. "Okay. Maybe I should ask you to sign something… like a non-disclosure agreement."

"Not only that, Jeremy, but you'll get rid of her right now. What are you thinking, having her in here? Are you so desperate for female attention that you called her and begged her to come see you?" Wow, nutcase much?

He scrunched his face up. "What? No! I need help, Mother. My solicitor quit, in case you hadn't noticed. Oh, that's right; you have noticed because you employed this idiot to take her place." He gestured at Mr Tubby, who breathed disdainfully through his nose. It made a high-pitched whine that was almost as bad as the noise made by nails tearing down a blackboard. My teeth tingled uncomfortably, and I shuddered.

"I don't have to put up with this, you know," he whinged. He turned to Jeremy's mother. "I can't work with another solicitor. Would you like me to walk?"

"Pfft, she's not a solicitor. She's a photographer. Goodness knows what she's supposed to be able to help him with." Catherine folded her arms and gave me a smarmy look, as if she was imagining exactly what I could help him with, and it wasn't getting him out of jail.

Jeremy stood. "I won't have you speaking to Lily like that. Get out!" He went to point with one finger, but his other arm got dragged up too, so he ended up pointing with both forefingers.

"Not until she signs a non-disclosure agreement." Catherine folded her arms. "Come on, Brian, get one here now. What am I paying you for?"

He hurried outside, then came straight back in, a document in his hand. "If you don't mind. It's just the standard agreement. Sign at the bottom." He placed it on the table. I picked it up and counted eleven pages.

"I'm going to read this first." I narrowed my eyes at both intruders. No one was bullying me into signing something I hadn't read. They looked at each other, both rolling their eyes. How old were these people? And one was supposed to be a solicitor? I gave Jeremy a sympathetic look. Now I knew why he needed me. He was dealing with idiots.

It took me fifteen minutes to read through—the legalese slowed me down. "I'm happy to sign, but you have to delete this clause first: *The signatory must disclose all evidence to Brian Pryor and Catherine Frazer and will not disclose any information to the accused, Jeremy Frazer.*"

"Let me see that." I slid it across to Jeremy, who read the page before it and then that page. His eyebrows drew down, thunder darkening his eyes. He spoke through clenched teeth. "I'm the client here, not my mother. If you can't understand that, you can leave now. I'll tell the PIB to ban both of you from visiting or contacting me."

Catherine pursed her lips. "I only want the best for you, Jeremy. If you want to get out of here, let us take care of things. You're too emotional right now to think straight."

"If you really loved me, you'd do as I ask right now."

She took a deep breath. "All right. You win. Give me that." She took the paper. "What would you like it to say, Son?"

"The signatory must disclose all evidence to Jeremy Frazer—the accused—and no other unless they have his express and detailed written approval."

His mother left the room, then came back with white and blue paper. She must have magicked two copies into existence after changing it to what he wanted. He read over the pages. "Thanks, Mum." His voice was even and cautious. He probably didn't want to provoke further confrontation. Being in here was stressful enough without adding family squabbling into it. "Here, Lily." He took a pen from his mother and handed it to me with the paper.

I read it too, just to make sure, then signed both of them. Now it was official—there was no going back. If he was guilty, I was in a major pickle, and I'd have hell to pay with Angelica and James. "Done."

"You can keep the white one. My solicitor can have the blue one." Jeremy smiled and looked at me. He turned back to his mother. "Now, if you wouldn't mind, we don't have much time left before I have to go back to my cell. Please leave, and take your shitty excuse for a lawyer with you."

"I'll be back later, Jeremy. Maybe I can make you see sense." His mother pinched her lips together and glared at me once more before turning and leaving. Mr Tubby followed her out and left the door open. How rude. I got up and shut it before sitting back down.

"Sorry about that, Lily." He lowered his face into his hands for a moment before sitting up again.

"How do you know he's incompetent?"

"After my mum hired him, I did some research—the PIB were kind enough to let me do that, at least. He's lost forty-eight out of his last forty-nine cases. He's a massive joke in law enforcement circles, apparently. He was so bad, he was fired by the government from his public prosecutions job."

"Wow, that is bad." Jeremy was so up against it, which was weird, considering he was famous and rich. "Where are all your friends? What about your agent?"

"None of my actor friends want to come near me. It's not true that bad publicity is still good publicity. A couple of them have called. They apologised for not coming to see me, but that's it. I haven't heard from my agent, and when I tried to call, she didn't answer." His shoulders sagged. I didn't blame him for feeling defeated. It brought back when pretty much everyone I loved had abandoned me. Not much sucked more than that—well, other than my parents disappearing.

"Right. Well, I want to ask you a couple more questions before we finish up, and please be honest with me. Okay?" I didn't want to go off on a wild goose chase.

"I promise I won't lie, Lily. Only the truth for you." His blue eyes bored into mine. Imploring me to believe him or trying to convey something more, I didn't know. I'd just have to take him at his word for now and not read other stuff into his gazes. I didn't want this to become awkward because of my overactive imagination. I wondered what Will was doing right at that moment. Was he in the building? Might I run into him in the corridor? I could hope.

Might as well cut to the chase. "Did you kill Trudie?"

He shook his head vehemently. "No."

"But you told me you hadn't seen her for years, and there was a photo of the two of you on the red carpet together two years ago."

He pressed his lips together. "Yes, well, that wasn't what it looked like. We'd both gone to the same event. She caught up to me—on purpose, of course—on the red carpet. There wasn't much I could do without looking like an arsehole in front of all the cameras, so I had to grin and bear it… literally. As soon as we went inside, I pushed her away and told her never to come near me again. I'm willing to swear my magic on it." Well, that was telling. I was betting that the vehemence in his voice was real and not put-on. That answered that question.

"Okay. And sorry for the next question, but I have to ask. Did you kill Amanda?"

He firmly shook his head. "No. I haven't killed anyone. Not. One. Person."

It hit me then. The reason I was helping him had been there all along, and I was too slow to see it. Talk about dense. I'd been falsely accused, and no one had believed me. Everyone was only too happy to treat me like a criminal before anything had been proven. I'd almost gone to jail for a very long time for something I hadn't done. I knew exactly what it was like to be in Jeremy's position. It was the worst. And I never wanted that happening to anyone else.

"Did you leave your gran's house after Trudie left?"

"No."

"Do you know anyone who has it in for you? Is there someone who wanted you out of the way or wanted to destroy you?" *Destroy* sounded rather melodramatic, but no one ruined a person's life because they'd been cut off in traffic. Whoever was out to get him wanted blood, and lots of it. What had he done to attract that kind of attention?

He chewed his top lip while he thought. "There's another actor, Aaron Hayze. Do you know him?"

"Yeah. He was in *Call to Mrs Valentine* and that stupid American comedy *Copping a Feel*." I rolled my eyes. It was such a stupid play on words. It was about a police officer who was a womaniser, but of course his one true love turned him around, and the "feels" he was going for turned into feelings. So original.

"Yeah, that's him. He was upset when I won Sexiest Man of the Year in *GQ Magazine*, and then when I won that Oscar, he went nuts. He took a drunken swing at me at one of the afterparties, threatened to do something to get me out of the way."

"Oh my God. That's crazy. What's wrong with people?"

He shook his head. "I have no idea. He's the only one I can think of right now who hates me."

"Well, only one person hating you is a good thing. Does he live in the US?"

"Yeah. California. He could be on set anywhere in the world right now though. He landed a spy movie. I heard they're filming some of it in Europe."

"Nice work if you can get it. Is he a witch?"

"Yes."

"Cool. I just need to know what I'm dealing with. Hmm...." I tapped my pen on my nose. "There was one other thing. Who was that guy who spat on you when you were arrested? He was yelling out some pretty hateful stuff."

Jeremy shook his head. "Just an idiot I went to school with—Douglas Marsh. He never liked me. We'd exchange words now and then, but I pretty much ignored him. He was a dweeb. I don't know... he hated me. I didn't like him but only because he wouldn't leave me alone. He was always hassling me for something. He had a massive crush on Amanda. He's sent me a couple of hateful letters since school. I used to think he was harmless, but now that I think of it, he threatened Amanda and I after we got together, said we'd regret it." His face tensed in a pained expression.

"You didn't bully him or anything? As in, he didn't have any other reason to hate you, did he?"

He half laughed. "No. I was too busy concentrating on my acting, even back then. I didn't have time to worry about whether some idiot liked or didn't like me. Especially the last three years of high school. I landed a few bit parts on TV, and when I was sixteen, I had six months shooting *Don't Look Now*. I had a tutor on set, but when it was done, I went back to my regular school to finish up. If anything, this has to do with Amanda." He sat up straight, alert. "Actually... Douglas's brother is a Kent police officer. He joined the force as soon as he left school, and he still was one a couple of years ago. I had to deal with him for a night-club opening I attended."

"Is he the kind of guy who would cover things up for his brother?"

He shook his head. "I honestly don't know. He and Douglas are close, but whether he'd jeopardise his career...?"

"Okay. Well, out of everyone, he seems like the most likely suspect." I left the "other than you" off the end. "Keep thinking on it. If you remember anything unusual about after Trudie left, or if you can think of anyone else who might want you out of the picture, let me know. If I can get some evidence on Douglas, maybe the PIB will question him."

"Thanks, and I'll think about it. If I remember anything

else, I'll call you." His smile was wan, but at least it was there. "Thank you for believing in me, Lily. You have no idea what it means."

I smiled. "I think I do, and I'm happy to help. But don't thank me yet. We have a long way to go, unfortunately." I stood, and so did he.

"Let me know straight away if you find anything."

"I will. See you soon." I gave a small wave and exited. One of the two PIB prison guards waiting outside asked if I was done. "Yep. I guess he can go back to his holding cell now." I looked back over my shoulder as sadness waterlogged my heart. Jeremy sat there staring at the table. With his messy hair, prison garb, and the weight of his conviction wilting him, he looked like a defeated man. There was nothing movie star about him right now. Could I change that for him? And if he wasn't the killer, who was?

"Lily? What are you doing here?"

What the—? I looked up. Will stood there, the agent he was spying on next to him. My eyes widened. "Ah… um…." I swallowed.

"Yes, indeed, Lily. What are you doing here?" I turned around. Angelica strode down the corridor, bearing down on me like the iceberg that sunk the Titanic. I looked from her to Will and back again. *Crap.*

I couldn't help my guilty look at Jeremy as the guards led him out of the interview room and down the hall.

"You're not serious!" My gaze snapped to Will, who had his hands on his hips. He looked over my head at Angelica. "Is she for real?"

"Yes, I'm afraid so." She turned her angry gaze on me. "I've just heard that you have agreed to help Mr Frazer clear his name. By the look on your face, I don't have to ask if it's true. What in all the magic in the world were you thinking? And you signed a non-disclosure agreement!"

My cheeks heated. I knew she wouldn't be excited about what I was doing, but to be this angry seemed out of proportion. It wasn't as if I'd killed anyone.

"How could you?" spat Will. "You're betraying the PIB by doing this and disrespecting Ma'am. I'm so glad I broke up with you. What you do reflects on all of us. You're making us look like a bunch of fools." The agent with Will smirked. All this was totally going to find its way back to Piranha. But how much of Will's scolding was real and how much was put-on?

As my gaze pinged from one side to the other, I felt like a tennis ball in a match between Federer and Nadal. Angelica's arms were crossed now. "Just wait till your brother finds out." She shook her head. "I'm extremely disappointed in you right now."

I swallowed. Tears sprang to my eyes, which totally sucked. I wasn't doing anything wrong. I was just trying to help someone, and if that meant I was the bad guy, then so be it. I bit my tongue, hard, drawing blood. At least the tears had retreated. I stood straighter and gave them each a scathing glare. "I'm helping an innocent man. I don't have to explain myself to either of you." I turned to Will. "And as for you, buddy, you broke up with me. I owe you nothing. Go cry about this to stupid Dana, the evil witch. I'm sure she'll *comfort* you." I spared an extra glare for her lackey; then I made a doorway around myself—dangerous, but it fit with the drama of the moment—and landed straight in Ma'am's reception room. I threw the door open and stomped up to my room, being sure to try and put my foot through each stair tread as I went.

Anger burnt my veins, turning my blood to steam. *How dare they speak to me like that?* I mean, Angelica wasn't even in on the breakup thing—her reaction was real, and if hers was all real, some of Will's had to be too. I magicked my shoes off and fell back-first onto my bed. I smooshed my pillow over my face and screamed my frustration until my throat was raw.

I sat up, acknowledging the rumble of fear deep in my belly. Was our pretend breakup real? And after seeing their reactions, what was James going to say? Would he be more my brother or more PIB agent? I sighed and wiped an errant tear from my eye. Well, as the saying went, I'd made my bed, but I wasn't going to lie in it doing nothing. It was time to get to work and prove everyone wrong, prove that Jeremy was innocent.

As I turned my laptop on, ready to research before I made my next move, I ignored the possibility that he was guilty. The repercussions didn't bear thinking about.

Oh boy, had I made my bed.

CHAPTER 13

I ate a Vegemite sandwich for lunch—you can take the girl out of Australia, but she'll still eat Vegemite. Okay, so that wasn't quite how that saying was supposed to go, but whatever. As soon as I was done, I called Jeremy's lawyer. I wasn't sure if he'd take my call, so I was happily surprised when he said, "Hello, Brian here."

"Hi, Brian. It's Lily, the person trying to help your client." I didn't think a bit of a reminder would go astray. He *was* supposed to be defending him.

"What do you want?"

Well, that wasn't very friendly. "I need to see the evidence files on the women Jeremy's accused of murdering. I want to know when and how they were killed, etcetera." Even though I'd seen the files at the PIB, I couldn't remember everything, and I hadn't seen everything on where and how they were discovered. If I wanted to get photographic evidence, I'd need to visit the places they'd been found. I planned on sneaking to the creek behind Jeremy's grandmother's later. I could probably ask her for access, but I didn't want her twigging about what my talent was. I mean, it would be hard to figure out since I didn't think anyone else had my type of talent, so why would you think it, but I needed to be careful, nonetheless.

"I don't think so. You're not a lawyer. You're probably working for the PIB. Even though you signed that document today, I don't trust you."

I growled under my breath. This was going about as well as I'd thought it would. "Okay, that's fine, but you won't mind when I put in a complaint and have you disbarred for not helping your client. Your track record is atrocious. Do you try and lose each case? Maybe someone's paying you to lose this one too?" Throwing out a few wild accusations couldn't hurt. Maybe he'd be stupid enough to believe them.

He coughed. "How dare you! Look, I don't have time for this."

"Fine. Don't say I didn't warn you."

Silence. Was he still there? Ah, there was some breathing. I smiled.

"By—"

"Okay, okay. You can see the police files. And this is no admission of guilt. It's not my fault I can't choose my clients well. If they don't want to do the time, they shouldn't do the crime."

My mouth dropped open. Oh. My. God. Why did

Catherine hire this idiot? "Great. I'll come by now. Can you have everything ready?"

"Yes, but none of it leaves my office. Understood?"

"That's fine."

"And you only get thirty minutes with the files. I'm going out, but my secretary will show you to my evidence storage room. You can look at it there. Good day, Miss Bianchi."

And that was that. I would walk up. His office was near Camille's old office—the woman who'd had an affair with Liv's ex-fiancé. The same woman who stole millions from unsuspecting retirees. Did Westerham have an unusual number of criminals, or was I just deluded as to the percentage of the world population who were dishonest? It was probably the latter. How depressing.

I magicked my shoes back on and left, camera in my bag. As soon as I had all the info, I was going to visit all the murder sites. There was no use wasting time. The sooner I got the evidence, the better. At least I'd have something to vindicate myself with when James came to tear me a new one… maybe.

Brian's office was in an old terrace, the white paint flaking off. A tiny sign next to the front door said Attorneys at Law, but his name wasn't on it. I rang the bell. A tall, lanky woman with curly grey hair and thick glasses opened the door. She didn't smile. "You must be that Lily woman Brian spoke of. Do that be you?"

Um, dobee dobee do. I choked back a laugh, and she scowled. Did she come from pirate land? "Um, yes, that's me."

She looked at her watch, then back at me. "You've thirty minutes and not a second more." Without waiting for my answer, she turned and walked back inside. I followed her, shutting the door behind me.

Fluorescent strip lighting illuminated the hallway, and the carpet was definitely from the 1970s—brown and swirly and stinking of smoke. The walls were yellowed, as were the light fittings. Ew. The realities of time travel were often ignored in movies. A romanticised version was always put forward, but what about this? A time when baby-poo green was fashionable in kitchens, and cigarettes—well, they practically gave them to babies when they popped out in hospital.

She took me to a small office at the back of the building that had a small window, covered by an ugly gauzy curtain, that looked out into the yard. The woman tapped her watch. "Twenty-eight minutes remaining." She turned and left.

Hmm, so friendly. I rolled my eyes. Okay now to ignore my shabby treatment and find what I needed. An office-type desk pushed up against one wall was covered by piles of paper. I had no idea where to start. Ooh, I remembered an awesome copy spell. I could just send a copy of all these to my bedroom and go through them in non-stinky surroundings. I smiled. "Copy each sheet, and make it neat. Deliver it to my bedroom at Angelica's, now." My face warmed as the spell worked. Oh, crap! I put my hand to my mouth. I forgot to buy paper. Had I just stolen it from the local office supply store? Was I now a criminal? I'd have to find out where it came from and pay them what it cost. Damn! When was I going to get used to witching?

The warmth faded away. Hopefully everything had gone to my room. I had a quick squirrel through the stuff on the desk. Some of it was utterly unimportant—receipts for a toaster and microwave that the police must have picked up when they raided his home—but here was one of the files I'd seen part of at the PIB. I took photos of each page with my phone, just in case my spell hadn't worked properly.

Maybe I should have a look around Jeremy's place too. If he'd committed any crime there, it would be apparent pretty quickly. I'd just assumed he lived with his grandmother when he was here, but of course, he probably had a flat in London or something. He was a grown man after all, and I couldn't see him still living with his horrible mother. She'd drive anyone mad. Although, where had he lived when all this started over ten years ago?

I ferreted around and found one more of the files I'd been looking for—the one on his dead girlfriend. I snapped shots of all of that too. Once I was done, I was going to go through more piles, but Brian's secretary came in. "Time's up!" She held her arm up and pointed to her watch. She moved her head like a chicken while scrutinizing the table. Maybe she was seeing if I'd moved anything? Or was she just curious as to what I'd been interested in? She looked me up and down. "Ye didn't be taking anything, did ye?"

"No, of course not! Everything is still here. You can check my bag if you like." Had I just lied? Well, not technically. I hadn't removed anything. I'd made new stuff. New stuff was not this stuff. I was letting myself off on a technicality.

"All righty then." She grabbed my bag and looked inside. What the hell? I know I told her she could, but seriously…. Satisfied, she handed it back. "Be away with ye now."

And just like that, I'd been dismissed. I couldn't be bothered walking back home, and since she'd been so rude, I didn't think it mattered if I left abruptly. "Goodbye," I said, then made my doorway, and stepped through. It wasn't until I was standing in my bedroom surrounded by thousands of papers that I thought to ask one important question: Was that woman a witch, or had I just freaked out a "normal" cranky old lady? Oops. I was witching so badly today—first stealing paper, then potentially outing witches to nonwitches, which was a punishable offence. Angelica was already angry with me; now wasn't the time to give her other stuff to hate me for.

I stopped admonishing myself—I could continue that later—and dug through the mess to find the rest of what I needed. Thankfully, it was all there. I spied some other interesting stuff, but it would have to wait. Maybe my photos at the crime scenes would show me exactly who the killer was.

I logged into the PIB site and checked out the places the bodies were found against witch toilet portals. One was within five hundred metres of a portal, but the rest were three–four miles from one. It would take less time to just drive, rather than walk from toilet cubicle to each site, plus the weather could change at any time, and I'd find myself in the pouring rain.

I chucked my knapsack into Angelica's car and set off. I couldn't help a little snicker—I was using her car to help me do something she didn't want me to do. Well, if justice wasn't her motive, bad luck. I'd rather look like an idiot, have people angry at me, and know I did the right thing than send an innocent man to jail to save face, which was what Angelica and Will were suggesting should happen. If I was honest with myself, I'd admit how disappointed I was with them. Did their attitude come from being jaded after years of dealing with evil, or was it they just couldn't imagine what it was like to be incarcerated when you were innocent? Well, I could, and I needed to do this, even if it made me about as popular as a swarm of mosquitos at a barbecue.

According to the files on each of the women, they weren't killed where they were found, and the police had never been able to identify where they'd been murdered. So many clues they didn't have. I crossed my fingers that the killer hadn't been careful when disposing of the bodies. My only hope was to get a picture of their face. According to the latest file, there were no traces of magic found at the crime scene, so whoever had killed Trudie had transported her the normal way. She'd been dumped at night, at a church down a country lane—no witnesses, no evidence except for tyre marks in the damp dirt next to the church grounds, which could have been left by anyone at any time. They'd noted two different tyre types, both common and likely belonging to a Volkswagen Polo and Mercedes-Benz A-Class.

Great, how fantastic.

Figuring out the car type the killer used was like finding a needle in a haystack—clichés existed for a reason; we all needed them sometimes. Hmm, could I rope Liv into helping me? I could really do with pulling the registration records of the guy who went to school with Jeremy. I didn't want to get her into trouble, but she was my only hope.

I dialled her number, my heart thudding noticeably from guilt at asking and fear that she'd be angry at me just like everyone else. But she didn't pick up. It went to messages. "You've reached Olivia. Sorry I can't answer right now. Please leave a message after the tone." *Beep.*

"Ah, hi, Liv. It's Lily. Not sure if you're even talking to me right now, but I really need your help with getting rego info on someone. Can you please call me back ASAP? Thanks." I hung up and sucked in a deep breath, letting it whoosh out loudly. Damn. There wasn't anything I could do about it right now, and I didn't want to waste any time. Jeremy was sitting in that stinking cell, and every minute would be torture. And how long could I stand everyone being angry with me?

I'd arranged the sites in order of where they were located in relation to Angelica's house rather than in order of when the bodies had been found. I wasn't even sure if the police had finished with the latest site, so I might have to visit that at night, when there would only be police tape and one half-asleep guard to stop me—okay, so that was an assumption on my part, but if they thought they had the murderer in custody, you wouldn't think too many people would be desperate to have a look. Plus, if the actual murder hadn't taken place there, they wouldn't need to spend so much time collecting evidence and taking photos.

My first stop was St Peter and St Paul's Church at Edenbridge, which was directly south of Westerham. The drive took just over ten long minutes. There was nothing like being by yourself in the car to overthink things. As much as I tried to block out thoughts of Will, they snuck in. Was he really angry with me, or was it all for show? I wanted to text him and find out, but that might blow his cover. Chances were, I'd text him and receive an angry rant in reply. My shoulders sagged. Why couldn't life be easy for five minutes? It seemed as if it was one depressing or dangerous day after another. There was little in the way of relaxation or pure joy. What the hell was up with that? Stupid universe.

I pulled up and parked in front of a quaint, greystone wall that marked the church property's front boundary. Tall trees spread their boughs behind the fence, their yellow leaves dotting branches and covering the ground. Across the road, brick semi-detached homes sat in a row, autumn-browned ivy trailing along some of the walls, tendrils framing aged timber windows.

I grabbed my camera and got out. The picture of the make-up artist was from here. She'd been placed amongst the graves that creepified the grounds between the fence and old stone church. I walked up the street and found a gap in the fence that was just to the right of the church. The path sat between graves. I turned and checked out the houses across the street and shuddered. Living across the road from a cemetery was the last place I'd want to live—you'd be the first to die in a zombie apocalypse, and surely your house would be haunted by bored ghosts who were looking for stuff to do at night.

Being curious and sometimes morbid, I didn't mind looking at headstones from over a hundred years ago to see what age people were when they died and what they'd died of, but today had a sharp edge to it. I was hunting a murderer and risking friendships to do it. There was also something else that raised my arm hair, a discomfort I couldn't name.

Hardly any of the grave markers were straight—most lurched one way or the other like a swarm of zombies. I whispered to myself and magicked the crime-scene photo to my chest. I reached inside my coat and pulled it out. Holding it up, I turned around, trying to match the headstones in the photo to the ones in the grounds. Hmm, was that it?

I walked closer to the church and veered left, to two rounded headstones that were next to a taller rectangular one. Broad branches from a huge pine hovered low over the graves, protectively, like a swan sheltering her young. I traversed the narrow space between headstones to get a closer look. "Sorry for treading on you…"—I leaned down and read the inscription—"Mavis. I hope you don't mind." She hadn't had a bad go. Died at seventy-two, but that was in nineteen fifty-six. That was a pretty good innings back then. Taking another gander at the photo confirmed it. "This is the spot."

I backed away a few metres so I could get more of the scene in the shot. Would it play out as a movie again? And did I have any control over it if it did? The video mode sapped my energy much more than just taking photos, just as it would if I were the camera battery. Excitement and worry seesawed in my stomach, first one shooting to the top, then the other.

I made the doesn't-really-sound-like-a-drumroll-but-I'm-trying noise with my tongue because I felt like this needed a drumroll. "Show me who killed the make-up artist." Darkness blackened my lens. A figure crouched, hands reaching for something on the ground, but the night had been so dark that the silhouette was only just showing up against the even darker background of the tree. Bummer.

I frowned and walked around to get a view from the other side, which meant I was jammed up next to the tree, looking back towards the street. The silhouette was a bit clearer this way because faint street lights shone behind. But there was no detail I could discern. I walked until I was face-to-face with the person in black. From closer, I could see they were of medium build, but since they were crouched, I couldn't tell their height, and they wore pants, jacket, and balaclava. There was no way I could even tell if the figure was male or female. Although, the person did look shorter than Jeremy. I crouched in the same position and tried to compare my slouching body length to theirs. Hmm, I was a bit shorter... maybe. It was hard to tell.

I stood and tried again. "Show me the killer arriving with the body." I scanned the street through my camera. It was so dark, despite the street lights, that I walked over to the fence and looked up and down. Nothing. Maybe it hadn't worked? Surely whoever it was hadn't travelled there, had they?

Turning, I focussed on the church. I made my way around to the doors, careful to check in real life where I was walking. The closer to the church I got, the darker it became, if that were even possible. I tilted my head back and looked up at the night sky, shrouded in clouds. No moon. No stars. No light. Nothing but black on black on black. I shivered, almost smelling the damp night air when I inhaled. Even though I knew it was really daytime, this was creeping me out, so I strayed closer to the church, straining to detect a person in the gloom.

And there it was. A shadow within the shadows, just outside the church doors. I still couldn't see any details, but I snapped some shots, showing they had travelled here, which was something, since they'd managed not to leave any magic traces on the body, although didn't James say they hadn't suspected witches, so the PIB hadn't been involved to test for that? Had they found any magic on Trudie? And if they had, would it be the remnants from slamming into Jeremy's invisible wall? Which would incriminate him all the more. Gah.

I approached the shadow, getting close enough to touch the killer. Whoever it was did look taller than me, and they seemed to be struggling under the weight of the dead woman slung over their shoulder. The killer's legs were bent and their back bowed. So we weren't dealing with a weight lifter. Jeremy was buff—yes, even I'd noticed in his latest movie when he took his shirt off—but he wasn't huge. Still, he was taller than the killer, and I wouldn't imagine he would be struggling quite so much—none of the murdered women were large. From the police reports, they ranged from about five foot three to five foot six, slim build, except for the mystery woman—she'd been medium build, but I couldn't remember the weight. Stupid brain. That guy from school who hated him probably weighed the same, but he looked to have more fat than muscle. Hmm. Something to ponder.

It was too dark to see anything else about the murderer, and at least I could assume the killer had travelled rather than driven. Did that mean they had to turn up earlier and set the landing spot? Interesting. I'd have to come back tomorrow when I could get inside. There was no way they would have been wearing a balaclava in the middle of the day when they set the landing spot. Maybe this wasn't going to be as hard as I'd thought. Nevertheless, I needed to check out the other murder scenes.

I turned my camera off and blinked in the daylight. It wasn't bright compared to a sunny Sydney day, but compared to what it had been, it was like looking directly into the sun. *You're getting soft, Lily.* I smiled to myself as I slid back into the car. Maybe I should try and plan a trip home soon. I missed the beach and my old friends—Skype video wasn't quite the same, and the lag made it annoying because we kept talking over the top of each other.

The next location was about twenty minutes' drive further south, to a tourist spot called Groombridge Place. I'd checked it out online, so I knew what to expect. It was a stunning 1660s brick manor house on a massive land plot. From the photos of the formal gardens and "enchanted forest," it was the sort of place I'd love to spend the day. Unfortunately, I was going there for an entirely unenjoyable reason. It was tricky since it was closed during the week, and the house was out of bounds to visitors, as it was lived in and used as a proper residence. The body had been left on a giant chess board—yes, that's right, a giant chess board. Why there was anyone's guess. The police were yet to agree on it. Was it random or a choice? From what I'd seen about serial killers on TV, they liked to toy with the authorities, so maybe it was some kind of cryptic clue.

The main entry gates to the road leading to the manor were shut. I'd expected it, and I could easily find a way to magic my way inside, but what if the people living or working there were witches? My no-notice spell would never work. Maybe I needed to do this when it was dark, as I'd done with Beren last night. I gritted my teeth in frustration. *Patience, Lily.* "Yeah, yeah, I know. Be patient. Easy for you to say." Yes, I was talking to myself—but don't judge. I'm not the only one, and you know it.

There was nothing that said I couldn't take photos from here. At least it would show me whether or not the killer had driven or magicked themselves over. I cast a no-notice spell

—even if the owners were witches, at least passers-by wouldn't stop and ask why I was taking photos of the front gates.

Standing near the main two-lane road and looking back at the grand iron gates, I said, "Show me the killer arriving with the body." I turned in a slow circle till I was facing the estate again. Nothing. They must have travelled here too. I turned my camera off and hopped in the car. Today was turning into a depressing waste of time. Meanwhile, Jeremy was locked in a tiny cell smelling toilet fumes. That was a punishment in itself. I scrunched my nose in remembrance, put my blinker on, and turned onto the main road.

My next stop was just over an hour to the northwest. It was a car park in the Surrey Hills area, near a place called Peaslake. How had they come up with such a silly name? Or was there actually a lake of peas. I could picture it, the gentle slope of grassy field to a lake filled with peas as far as the eye could see, like those children's ball pits but way squishier. But wait a minute! Brits loved mushy peas, didn't they? I laughed. Was there a potato hill and carrot marsh? Maybe all those years ago, they'd had rules, kind of like when you were on Facebook and a meme says, you're in a zombie apocalypse. The thing closest to you is your weapon. What is it? The local priest probably rushed in and said, "Lord Busby, we need to name that damn lake before tomorrow's festivities." Lord Busby looked down, and, luckily, his dinner plate was sitting there. "I'll just use the first food I put in my mouth at dinner. Peaslake it is!" Little did they know that their methodology would re-emerge in the future when important things such as "what's your porn-star name" and "what's your zombie-apocalypse weapon" were in danger of not being figured out. It was incredible how far society had come….

Thirty minutes into my drive, sleepiness tugged at my eyelids. It must be coffee time. "Hey, Siri, where is the nearest Costa Café?" I didn't know if there was one nearby, but if there was, I was in.

Siri's happy voice came from my phone. "The nearest one I found is Costa, which averages five stars. Does that one sound good?"

"Yes."

"Perfect. I can call that location or get directions. Which would you like?"

"Directions, thanks." I giggled at how ingrained being polite was. Siri was a computer, not a person, yet I treated her like one.

"Getting directions to Costa." She switched over to map mode and told me how to get there. Technology was incredible, so much so that why did people think witches were an impossibility? So much stuff we took for granted was science-fiction stuff, and even though it existed, I had no idea how it could. Maybe it didn't take much to confound me, but still, the world was an amazing place.

With Siri's awesome guidance, I found Costa, grabbed a coffee and sandwich, and got back in the car. I sat there and enjoyed my afternoon snack while trying not to think about everything I had going on. I was pretty sure I'd earned five minutes of mental peace.

My phone rang.

Okay, maybe not.

Instead of seeing the name I wanted on the screen—Olivia—it was James. I so wanted to let it go to message bank, but then I'd just have an angrier brother to deal with later. I swiped to answer. "Hello, brother of mine." Maybe reminding him we were related would make him be nicer?

His voice was so loud, I had to hold my phone away from my ear. "What the hell were you thinking, agreeing to help a serial killer and signing a non-disclosure?!" Or maybe not. There were a lot of maybe nots happening to me today. If only I could fast-forward to tomorrow.

I rubbed my temples with thumb and middle finger. "Do you remember when stupid Snezana kidnapped you?"

"Yes, but what has that got to do with the price of fish?"

"I told you the story about how I spent time in jail, did I not? And where would I and, for that matter, you be if no one had believed in me and helped me? I'm not an idiot, and don't think I haven't considered the fact that he might be guilty. If he's innocent, not only does he not deserve to be in jail, but the real killer is still out there. If he's guilty and I find evidence, I'll find a way to drop you a hint. Okay?"

He was silent for a few beats, but I wasn't going to gush into it and try and appease him. I needed to do this, and if he didn't understand why, that was his bad luck. "Argh! All right, fine. But if you find evidence proving he's guilty, I want to be the first to *get the hint*."

"Of course."

"Where are you?"

"Sitting in Angelica's car outside Costa."

"Why didn't you just walk?"

I smiled. "I'm not in Westerham. This Costa is a bit far to walk to."

"Are you going to tell me where you are?"

I didn't see the harm in it. It wasn't as if he was going to pop over here and drag me home. *Actually, knowing James, he just might.* "On the way to Peaslake, actually."

"You wouldn't be going to a certain car park, would you?"

"Maybe."

"Well, be careful. I mean it, Lily. I think you're wasting your time, but don't forget Dana's out there somewhere, and if you're right, so is a serial killer who wants your friend in jail. Oh, and Will's not very happy about you helping the guy either."

I rolled my eyes. "Yeah, he made that clear this morning, but guess what? We've broken up, and he doesn't get a say." I knew I was splitting hairs—he still cared about me, and we'd still be together if it wasn't for our investigation into Regula Pythonissum. But for some stupid reason, I felt rejected, and I was annoyed. Also, having been single for so long, I wasn't used to having to consider other opinions on what I did or didn't do. That was a hard habit to break, and maybe I didn't want to break it.

"Yeah, well, just tread lightly, Lily. I'll speak to you later."

"Okay, bye."

"Bye."

At least that hadn't been as bad as I'd thought it was going to be. Interesting to know Will was so angry that he'd ranted to James. Which meant his anger at me was 100 percent real—it wasn't an act to fool Dana's associate.

I downed the last of my coffee. Time to get going. I pulled into traffic and noticed a small white car down the street pull out at the same time. There was something familiar about it. Hmm, was that paranoia talking after my phone call with James? I mean, of course a small white car looked familiar—there were thousands of them on the road. I shook my head. *Get a grip, Lily.*

As I made my way out of the town under Siri's guidance, I continually checked my rear-view mirror. The car was still there—three cars back. It was plausible that they'd be going the same way if they were leaving the village too, and this *was* the main thoroughfare. Ten minutes later, they were still there, four cars behind me. Right. Maybe I would laugh at myself later, but for now, I'd listen to my gut. A left turn I wasn't supposed to make came up, and at the last possible minute, I slammed on the brakes and indicated, before hurtling around the corner. The car behind me beeped as it passed the street I'd turned into. *Yep, sorry.* It was a crappy thing for me to have done, but I was sure they'd forgive me if they knew why.

Fifty metres down the street, I pulled over and waited to see if that car turned too. Yep, there it was. And there it went, passing me without slowing. I didn't get a great look at the driver—the windows were tinted, and I was pretty sure they had sunglasses and a hat on. I couldn't even tell if it was a man or a woman. But now they'd probably know I was onto them. Should I continue to the car park, or should I just go home? Stuff it. I was still going to go. There was plenty of daylight left, and I felt safer in it. Plus, they'd kept driving down the street until I couldn't see them anymore.

I turned the car around and made a left back onto the main road. The rest of the trip was incident and stalker free, if, indeed, there had even been a stalker. Eventually, I reached the Surrey Hills Area of Outstanding Natural Beauty. The body had been found well into the forested locale, in a car park called Reynards Hill. The narrow road begrudgingly fit two cars. Trees and bushes flanked the bitumen, birds swooping from branch to branch. I would have opened my window to listen to them twittering, but it was too cold.

The road turned to dirt just as I reached the end of the journey—the car park—which was just a cleared circular area surrounded by forest. I parked the car and waited for a moment, just in case the white car turned up. Thankfully, nothing. Fine. I'd probably imagined the whole thing.

I turned my camera on and got out, positioning myself at the entry to the parking area. I magicked the crime-scene photo straight to my hand this time—I was the only one here, and I didn't think the birds would mind. The air smelled of decaying leaves and ozone. I looked up through the leafy canopy. The intermittent clouds of earlier had banded together and darkened, promising rain in the next hour. Visiting the fourth crime scene tonight would totally suck if it was raining, but then again, maybe it would be easier to access. Whoever was guarding it would likely be staying in their car and watching from there, which would mean my no-notice spell would be enough. I'd just have to park a little bit away from the place and walk—I didn't know if I had the power to cast the spell on a moving vehicle and keep it there while I got out and wandered around cloaked in the same spell.

Swallowing my need to gag, I compared the photo to the car park. I didn't think it was possible to ever get used to the brutal images of ripped-off faces and missing hearts, no matter how many times I looked at these. According to the gory picture, the killer had dumped her body right at the end, amongst the trees. I jogged to where dirt met grass and undergrowth. The body had been found a few metres in. After a quick perusal, I hurried back to the road just outside the area and pointed my camera into the car park. "Show me the killer arriving with the body."

My breath caught in my throat, and I had a coughing fit. Oh my God, this was it. Yes, it was night-time and dark, but not as dark as when I'd been at the church. It was a white car, but larger than the one that'd followed me. I got closer to the back of it and took photos. It was a Skoda, and I couldn't believe my luck, but the number plate was visible… only just, but, hey, I'd take anything I could get. Even a partial number plate would be valuable.

GO08 PMS. I focussed in close and snapped. Then I went around to the front of the car and took more photos. It was too dark to see much detail about who was inside, but their silhouette was a little clearer than at the church. I placed myself a couple of metres from where her body had been dumped and said, "Show me the killer."

The killer stood over the body, hands on hips. The person was dressed in black and wore a balaclava again. When I went around to the front, I couldn't tell much more. I took some photos anyway, with the car in the background, and then lowered my camera. I had no desire to get a closer look at the body, and it wasn't as if I was going to find any evidence the police hadn't.

Uneasiness tightened the air. Whether it was my imagination or something was wrong, it was clearly time to leave. I took one last look at the place, letting the gravity of past events sink deep into my bones, then jumped back in the car, and headed home.

THE HOUSE WAS EMPTY WHEN I ARRIVED. WEARY FROM ALL the driving, arguments, and circling thoughts, and cold from, well, English weather, I spent time defrosting in a hot shower. When I was done, I called Liv again. Bloody message bank. I sighed and left another message. "Hey, Liv. If you can get info on a number plate, I'd really appreciate it. It's gee oh zero eight pee em ess. Oh, ha ha, PMS. Anyway, I'll give you a year's supply of your favourite tea if you'll help me with this. Bye." What were the chances she was really busy rather than avoiding my calls? The possibility stung, but I still had so much work to do. Every extra minute I took to solve this was an extra minute poor Jeremy was in jail.

The paperwork in my room beckoned. I sifted through some of it, hoping for clarity, but I had to admit it drew a strong case against the actor. The only thing I couldn't figure out was motive. I shook my head. He wasn't a psycho, so he'd need a pretty good motive to kill and mutilate someone—not that there could ever be any motive for mutilation—and it just wasn't here. Killing these women gave him nothing—not freedom, not money, not fame, since he was already famous, and probably not pleasure. Could he be someone who got their rocks off by killing someone? And where did getting your rocks off come from anyway? There were no rocks involved in a normal person's love life, and I couldn't see how you'd want there to be. Me and my stupid tangents. Anyway....

My phone rang, and I jumped. Talk about highly strung. The number was familiar. Oh, the prison section of the PIB. "Hello, Lily speaking."

"Hi, Lily. It's me, Jeremy. They're letting me have a phone call. I wanted to know if you could come see me." He sounded hesitant, so unsure of himself—this was not the confident guy I'd met only a few days ago. If his jail experience had been anything like mine, I could understand why.

"Of course. I can update you on the stuff I found today. Should I come now?"

"Yes, please." He heavy sighed. "I'll see you soon... and thanks."

"See you soon, and it's my pleasure. Hang in there, Jay."

Within a few seconds, I was buzzing the PIB reception-room door. Looked like Gus's shift was over because another taller, leaner guy answered it. He was probably about ten years younger than Gus too, with a shaved head and dark goatee. He stood at the door, blocking my way. "Name and reason for your visit."

"Lily Bianchi. I'm here to see Jeremy Frazer, one of the people in your cells."

"Place your hand here, please." He held up a thing that looked like an iPad, but it was all white. I put my palm on the device and warmth crept through it, stopping at my wrist. He pulled it away and writing popped up on the screen. "Okay. I'll take you down there."

"Ah, what was that?"

"Part of our new security procedure. It checks your magic signature against our database. Just confirming who you are, miss."

"Oh, okay."

He took me down corridors and lifts, another check-point, and then to the interview room I'd seen Jeremy at earlier. He didn't look any worse since yesterday, but certainly not better, except for the smile that materialised as soon as I walked through the door. "Lily, boy am I glad to see you."

"Are they treating you okay?" That sounded like a line from a movie, and I giggled.

"What's so funny?"

"I just feel like we're spouting movie lines. Stupid of me to laugh. I know how shitty it is in here. Sorry."

"No, not at all, and you make a fair point. If only it *was* a movie. So, what exciting facts have you found that are going to clear my name?" His blue-eyed puppy-dog gaze melted my heart. If only I had good news to share. He must have seen the look on my face because some of his hope died.

I bit my lip. I could try and soften the blow, or I could just get it out there. Meh, who was I kidding? I was the Band-Aid ripper offer. "I visited a couple of the places the bodies were found. I didn't get much at the first site because it was—" I stopped and blinked. Oops, almost gave my talent away. *Proceed with caution, idiot.* "Ah, there wasn't much to see, really. The second site was locked up. The body was found on a chessboard at Groombridge Place." He gasped, and his face paled. "Are you okay?" It wasn't as if he didn't know, was it?

He dropped his head, eyes closed. "I'll be okay."

"But didn't you know? I mean, at the time they found her, you were here. Surely the police told you they found your girlfriend's body at Groombridge."

He slowly raised his head. Tears glistened in his eyes. "I knew that, but not about the chessboard. It was our favourite thing to do. We'd been there twice. We joked we'd get married on it." He wiped his tears away with the palms of handcuffed hands. "We were in love, Lily. I never would have killed her. She was going to come to America with me, be my assistant. I'd earned enough that I had money to support both of us for a year or two, and I had offers coming in for TV shows and movies. Losing her broke my heart so bad that I haven't been in love since. I still have nightmares about it." He shook his head and just looked at me, sadness seeping from every pore.

Gah. I wanted to give him a hug, but that might be weird, so I didn't, but seeing him so devastated just proved to me that he was innocent. "I can't imagine how horrific it is to be in here and blamed for her death. But hang in there. I found some evidence at the forest car park, where they found the woman they couldn't identify. How did they nail this on you?"

"After charging me with Trudie's death, they obviously saw similarities with all of them. They could tie me to the make-up artist and Amanda, but the other woman was because of the condition of the body." He swallowed and shut his eyes momentarily.

"Yeah, those pictures are shocking."

He nodded and opened his eyes. "They showed them to me. Bastards." A tear spilled over onto one cheek. "I vomited when I saw the picture of Amanda. The way she died. It's just wrong, and I failed her."

"It's not your fault."

"But I should be able to protect the woman I love, don't you think? What a bloody failure I was. Maybe I deserve to be in here."

"Don't give up now, Jeremy. You were happy enough when I met you. And if Amanda loved you, she wouldn't blame you or want you to forfeit a happy life because of it. I'm sorry to ask again, but was there any other reason they linked you to that stranger's body?"

He sniffed and wiped his eyes again. "She was a fan, apparently. I didn't remember seeing her, but I'd had an event, and she was photographed in the crowd. They found a signed photo of me in her pocket. I'd signed it, *with love, Jeremy*. I don't even remember signing it, but it's my writing, my signature. But, you know, at these events, I can sign a couple of hundred photos, posters, whatever. Every face blurs into one after a while. I can't say that I didn't sign it. But even if I had, how does that mean I killed her?"

"They just wanted a link to tie you to all three, and that note provides it. So, the number plate I found out about—are you sure it won't be yours?"

"I didn't have a car at that time. I sold it because I was about to go to the US." Well, that was promising. "But how did you find a number plate, Lily?"

"Um, that's classified information. I'm sorry I can't tell you. But you can't tell anyone yet either." Shit, how had I not seen that coming. My IQ was dropping by the day. *Idiot.* "If it leads to something, the PIB will have to drop your case, so just bear with me. Please don't tell your mother or that buffoon you have representing you."

"But if it gets to court, can we?"

"Ah, I'm not sure. If it gets to court, it won't make any difference. If I find out who owned that car, I'm pretty sure I can find out who the killer is. But in the meantime, I'm going to check out Trudie's crime scene tonight. I'll let you know tomorrow if I find anything. Okay?"

He gave a sad smile. "Thank you." He barked a quick laugh. "I know I keep saying it, but honestly, you're the only person who believes in me. My own mother's been hinting I need to get used to the idea of being in here. She said it doesn't look good, and I shouldn't get my hopes up." He rolled his eyes.

"Wow, way to support you. I know she's your mum, but what a bitch. I'm sorry you didn't get a mother you deserved."

A knock sounded on the door. I swivelled around. The red-haired woman who'd been guarding the door when I arrived poked her head in. "Visiting time's up, miss. Let's go."

I turned back to Jeremy. A flash of panic glinted from his eyes before he got hold of himself and calmly stood. He tilted his head to the side and gave me such an earnest grateful-yet-sorrowful look that my heart felt as if it had just freefallen down a mountain. I was about to leave him to a scary, lonely night in jail, thoughts of his beloved deceased girlfriend roaming the darkened hallways of his memories.

I hurried over to him and gave him a bear hug. I felt way more comfortable with him than I should. Were we becoming friends? "Hang in there, Jay. I'll keep going till I get to the bottom of this. I promise."

"Thanks, Lily. I wish I could hug you back, but handcuffs."

"Yeah, I know. I hope you don't mind. I just thought you could use one."

"You thought right. This is the nicest hug I've ever had. I don't think I've ever needed one more. You're an amazing woman." He pressed his cheek against the side of my head for emphasis, I supposed.

"I said, let's go!"

"Yikes. I'd better leave before they arrest me too."

I pulled back, and he smiled. "Maybe you could keep me company." He winked, more of the Jeremy I'd met before this whole crap went down. I returned his smile and went to the door... which contained a scowling, arms-folded cranky-pants agent.

"What the hell are you doing? Fraternising with the inmates? Are you dating him now? I should have known you'd be seduced by fame. What, an agent isn't good enough for you anymore?"

"What the hell? We aren't even dating, and for your information, he's innocent. He's about to be put back in a cell and be miserable all night because he's still grieving his girlfriend after all these years, but because I show him a small kindness, I'm suddenly dating him? Look, Will, I get why we had to break-up, and I'm trying to deal with it the best I can, but I'm not ready to move on with anyone." I hoped he'd get through his thick skull what I was trying to say without saying, we're still together really, and as if I'd forget that. He winced. Good.

"Right, well, watch it. You're risking the PIB's reputation right now. I can't imagine James is too happy."

"No, he's not, but at least he's keeping his mind open to what I'm doing and not accusing me of anything." I folded my arms and raised one brow.

He took his scowl up a level. If he dialled it up any

further, he'd probably explode. He narrowed his eyes and pointed at me. "Just know I'm watching you, Lily. If you get into trouble, don't expect the PIB to bail you out. You're walking a fine line taking up with a murderer."

"He hasn't been convicted, last time I checked." I slammed my hands on my hips and bit my tongue to stop tears of frustration and insecurity from forming. Why was Will taking this so far? Whatever we were doing to fool Dana didn't need this drama too. As I'd surmised earlier that day, it seemed as if he was genuinely angry.

Someone bumped into my elbow. Ah, crap—Jeremy had heard Will's insults. The guard was leading Jeremy past me. He'd knocked into me on purpose as they walked down the corridor. He looked back and gave me a wan smile. He knew I had his back, but he didn't know how much it was costing me.

And to be honest, neither did I.

CHAPTER 14

I hadn't wanted to hear any more from Will—a girl could only take so much—so I'd made a doorway and skedaddled straight out of the PIB. It was dark by the time I got home, so I lit the fire in the lounge room and magicked myself some pumpkin soup for dinner. Angelica had bought a crusty loaf of bread yesterday, and I cut a generous chunk of that too. And politeness be damned—I ate it sitting in an armchair in front of the fire. It had been such a crappy day, and I was done caring about the people who were angry with me. I felt like my only friend was an actor I hardly knew who was stuck in jail for potentially being a serial killer. Was this really me living my best life? Epic fail.

After dinner, I magicked my spoon and bowl clean and into the cupboard—God, I loved being a witch when it came to housework—and then magicked my black clothes back on. This time I included a beanie because it was about five degrees out there and raining. Brrr. Not something to look forward to, but sometimes you had to pull up your big girl pants and get on with it.

I put some plastic over my Nikon so it wouldn't get wet —leaving a gap for the lens and viewing hole—grabbed my bag, which had the crime-scene photo inside, and trotted downstairs. I needed Angelica's car again, which meant driving in the atrocious weather. Unfortunately, I was leaving before I'd had a chance to see Liv. Surely she wasn't avoiding me on purpose? Maybe she'd had stuff on after work or had to work late. Yep, that must be it. Positive thinking was what I needed right now. Getting down on myself wasn't going to help me or Jeremy.

I sprinted the short distance from the house to the car, the freezing rain biting my face and neck. Gah, I should have worn a scarf. Oh, I still could. I grinned. Being a witch had its great points. Once I was snug in the car, I magicked my scarf to myself, right onto my neck. How skilled was that? Out of all the things I could do with my magic, this had to be one of the most satisfying, which was probably crazy of me, but whatever. Being a forgetful person, magic was making my life a lot less disappointing because when I left the house without something I needed, it didn't matter.

I had a forty-minute drive ahead of me, northwest. St James's Church in Cooling, the place where Trudie's body had been found, was a quaint little church on a small plot in a rural setting. The village only had a few hundred people, if that, and my Google search earlier today showed it was surrounded mostly by fields. There was a house on one side, but that was it. I plugged my phone into the car charger and punched in the address. At least I'd have Siri's company on the trip. Let's not get into how pathetic that was. I started the engine, then turned right out of my driveway.

The drizzle of earlier had turned into steady rain, and fifteen minutes into my trip, it increased to a downpour. I switched the radio off—it was that or turn it to near-deafening levels to drown out the thrum pounding on the car roof and the thunk, thunk, thunk of windscreen wipers. I drove below the speed limit, leaning forward, straining my eyes to see better. My jaw ached from my back teeth being jammed together with the stress of concentration. I probably should have done the drive in the daytime, set a landing spot, and travelled there tonight. Live and learn. Although, I'd never set one before, and I'd probably do something wrong and end up in the middle of a field ankle-deep in mud, or on someone's roof, or in the middle of the road just in time for a car to hit me. Yikes. Okay, so driving was probably the way better option.

My phone rang, and I started. Gah, I needed stress management classes. My damn phone was going to give me a heart attack one day. "Hey, Siri, answer the phone on speaker."

"Answering the call on speaker." *Thanks, Siri.*

"Hey, Lily, it's Imani. I'm just checking you're okay."

"Hi, Imani! I'm fine, thanks. How are you?"

"All right, love. I just had a weird feeling and wanted to check on you."

"I'm driving in the rain, but other than that, I'm safe."

"Oh, where are—" The phone crackled, and whatever else she said came out garbled.

"Hello? Imani, can you hear me? Imani?" No answer. Gah, stupid connection. It was so spotty on these country roads. The line finally cut out altogether. No gobbledegook. Nothing. Well, at least she knew I was okay, and I didn't have the brain power to call her back while navigating these narrow, slick roads. The tightness in my chest loosened a tad when Siri announced my destination was coming up on my right. I slowed. I was going to drive past the church and check out the guard situation, then turn around, drive back, and park towards where I'd originally come from. There were a few spots cut into the area off the side of the road.

Just before the road dog-legged to the left, around the church, my headlights shone on the side of a parked police car, revealing the silhouette of someone inside. The car was parked parallel to the church's fence and partly blocking a farm driveway. Yes! As much as running about in the freezing rain wasn't going to be fun, the weather had provided the best outcome—I was less likely to be noticed. I couldn't know whether the person in the car was a witch or not, so my no-notice spell might not be effective. The cover of rain would hopefully be just as good. I was sure whoever was in the car didn't expect anyone to be wandering about tonight and hopefully wasn't paying much attention. With some luck, they were having a nap.

There was a quick right turn as the road snaked around

the church. A row of trees obscured most of St James's, but I caught glimpses of it as I crawled past.

I drove down the road for a bit before finding a place to turn around. As I did that, I cast my no-notice spell—I should be out of range of police detection. The perfect parking spot sat about fifty metres from St James's, right in front of a vacant plot of land. It may have belonged to one of the houses next to it. It was hard to tell in the dark. Across the road, fields sprawled into the darkness. No wonder the killer had chosen this place to dump the body— it was unlikely you'd run into someone in the middle of the night.

I wrestled my raincoat out of my bag. Oh, crap. It was bright yellow. Of course it was. *Idiot, Lily.* I couldn't wear that. Angelica had a clear one. I should have thought to borrow it, but now I couldn't magic it to me because I didn't know exactly where it was—she could be wearing it for all I knew—and I didn't want to use magic, just in case anyone nearby was a witch and picked up on it. I shook my head at my stupidity. It seemed it was never-ending. Shame there was no spell to make it go away. I knew a few people who could have used an anti-stupidity spell too.

Time to suck it up. I'd be done in ten minutes, and then I just had to brave a five-minute drive before I could dry my clothes magically, right? I gave myself a firm nod, grabbed my camera, and hopped out.

I ran, head down, through puddles that drenched the lower part of my legs. Gumboots would have been good. Note to self: plan better next time. Goosebumps popped up along my arms, and I shuddered. There was only one street light shining from across the road and no light coming from the church—creepy much?

I climbed the low stone fence and carefully picked my way through headstones, my breath misting in the cold. I headed towards where the body had been found—behind a bush that was about halfway from the fence to the stone church. Yellow-and-black police tape cordoned off the area from there to the church in a wide arc. CRIME SCENE — DO NOT ENTER repeated along the tape. The law-abiding citizen in me was all too willing to obey, but I had to do what I had to do. I'd already broken the law a couple of times this week; what was one more? And there it was, the slippery slope we were all so close to sliding down. As I ducked under the tape, I wondered how much further down the law-breaking hill I was going to slide before this was over.

I lifted my camera and turned it on. "Show me the killer dumping Trudie's body." The image that materialised wasn't as dark as the previous ones, and in fact, there was more light in the picture than I had in real life. Still dressed in black and with a balaclava covering the face, there was nothing obvious about the person with their arms hooked under the victim's underarms, as they set Trudie's body down. The killer was at the victim's back, facing the church. I snapped some shots, then moved my camera from my face so I could check the ground out. There wasn't much to see in the dark, but it looked as if Trudie had been dragged at least part of the way to this spot.

I raised my camera again. "Show me the killer again." This time, the killer was standing above the body, gloved hands on hips. I really wasn't having much luck, but maybe I could get the PIB to check out whether they had any gloves in evidence. If Jeremy had been the killer, chances were, he'd still have the gloves. If they couldn't find any at his place, maybe that would be a point in his favour.

Something caught my attention. Oh. My mouth dropped open. I could see the killer's shoes, and this time, they weren't sneakers, or boots, or anything gender-neutral. They were dark court shoes, women's shoes with a low heel. I zoomed in and clicked.

"I don't know what you hope to find, missy photographer, but you've just snapped your last shot." I froze, recognising the voice.

Whatever came next, I couldn't have anyone discovering my photos. I turned and whispered, "Camera of mine, go back home, to the dining-room table, where someone will find you alone."

I was about to mumble a return-to-sender spell, but I was too late. A vortex gripped me, and St James's disappeared. Nausea scrambled up my throat, and just as I was about to give in to it, I was falling through the air. As I slammed into the hard ground, pain sliced through my arm and head, but it wasn't for long because everything faded to black.

CHAPTER 15

"Wake up, Lily," the voice whispered.

I groaned. Pain squeezed sharp, relentless fingers around my head. The nausea I'd blacked out to was still there but seemed minor in comparison to my headache. I lay on my side, on something uncomfortably cold and hard.

"Lily? I need you to wake up. Please." The voice was near to tears. Was I in hospital? No—no hospital bed was that uncomfortable, unless I was already dead and on a slab in the morgue. The person sniffed, then said, "If you're awake, please answer me." Did I have amnesia? I didn't recognise the woman's voice, but surely I knew them if they were that upset that I wasn't waking up. Plus, she knew my name. I supposed I could just open my eyes and find out.

I blinked. Light came from a lamp across the room, but

it wasn't bright, which was a good thing. But... I was viewing it through bars. I gasped. What the—

"Oh, thank God you're awake." The voice came from behind me. I slowly shifted to my back and to my other side. Um, I was in a cage, surrounded by steel bars. I reached out to touch them, confirm I was seeing what I was seeing.

"Don't touch them!"

I stopped and looked up. Holy crap, this wasn't good. Well, maybe it was good because if you were going to be locked in a cage, you may as well have company. Jeremy's first solicitor, Florence, sat in a cage next to mine. So that's where she'd disappeared to. "Um, you picked a weird place for a holiday." I didn't smile, but at least my sense of humour was trying. Not much was truly broken in my brain, it seemed. The pain was probably nothing a couple of ibuprofens couldn't fix. The cage was another matter.

"The bars are magicked to give you an electric shock if you touch them or try and perform any magic."

"Ah, like the PIB ones." I considered sitting up, but the way I felt, I'd need to lean back on something, and, well... not happening.

"Why are you in here? You didn't have much to help Jeremy's case."

Last time she'd seen me, I was a witness. I'd need to tell her everything that had transpired, but first, I needed to confirm who'd put us here. "I didn't really get a good look, but I recognised her voice last night. It's Jeremy's mother, isn't it?"

"Yes. Jeremy's innocent. Look over there."

There was a steel table, like the ones you'd see in an operating room, and, above that, three rows of steel shelves that ran half the length of the brick wall. I squinted my eyes, shut them, opened them, blinked, but nope, I was seeing what I was seeing. "Oh, my God," I whispered. So many emotions exploded within me at once: fear, anger, disbelief, and absolute horror. My mouth went dry, the moisture moving to my palms, making them sweaty and clammy. "Sweet, sweet, Jesus."

Jars lined the bottom shelf, which sat just above the height of the table. Hearts suspended in liquid were visible through the glass containers. On the shelf above the jars, one for each jar, was a row of busts that would normally be used as hat stands. Vomit shot to my mouth. I sat up quickly and made it to the edge of my cage in time, depositing dinner onto the concrete floor. "I'm so sorry." I wasn't sure if I was apologising to Jeremy's lawyer for the vomit or if I was apologising to the victims whose faces stared back at me from those busts.

Our own private horror movie.

"How are they so lifelike? They don't look dead."

"Magic. Catherine's put some kind of spell on them."

"But why? Why would she do this?"

A door squeaked open, and footsteps clicked on the floor. "Why, indeed," Catherine's smug voice replied. "You stupid bitches come sniffing around my boy, but you can't have him. He's mine. I gave birth to him, nurtured him, gave him everything. It broke my heart that he wouldn't stay here by choice, so I had to make him. He has yet to learn that Mother knows best. Now everything he has is mine. Including you." She smiled, lunacy blazing from her eyes. It was then I noticed she was wearing a plastic apron and gumboots. Wasn't that what butchers wore to work?

Adrenaline flooded my body. My breaths came quicker, and my heart raced—but my flight or fight response was wasted. All I could do was sit in my cage and glare.

Catherine laughed. "Oh, poor, poor photographer. I'm crying for you, boo hoo. I saw the way you watched my son, salivating, waiting to get your claws into his fortune. You only have yourself to blame… oh, and Jeremy. If he knew how to keep it in his pants, we wouldn't have this problem, but he just doesn't listen to his mother. And that stupid Amanda. I cared for her in the beginning, lovely girl she was. She promised if I supported their relationship, she'd get him to stay, but then I discovered they were going to move to the US. That whole thing was upsetting, to say the least. Now he's in jail, he'll have a long time to think about what he's done wrong." She shook her head and tut-tutted. How had Jeremy turned out so normal, nice even, after having this evil witch as a mother? Maybe he was adopted.

"I'm so disappointed in both of you. I'd thought you'd have more to say for yourselves." I had a lot to say, but I didn't think it would make any difference. I could stick up for her son, myself, Florence, but she would just argue. Although, the longer we kept her talking, the less time she had to rip our hearts out and faces off. Maybe it would give me time to think of some way to get out of here.

"What can I say, other than you're right. You got me. I

loved that Jeremy was famous and had lots of money. Photography's a hard gig to make money out of—so much competition and all that. He's lucky to have a mother like you to look out for him." Thank goodness Pinocchio wasn't a real thing, because my nose would be sticking a foot out of the cage by now.

She narrowed her eyes. Why couldn't she be stupid as well as crazy? "Really, you're changing your tune so quickly? You denied you liked him before."

"Look, I don't like confrontation. I didn't want Marcia to cancel me from the shoot, so I lied and said I didn't like Jeremy, but the moment I met him, I wanted him. I mean, good-looking, famous, and rich? Sign me up." I smiled through the pounding in my head. And to think, some women were really like this.

Catherine walked past my cage and stood in front of Florence's. "And then there's you, Miss Hotshot Lawyer. Not only did you want to sleep with my son and leave your taint on him, but you were going to charge him four-hundred pounds an hour. I won't have my son wasting his money like that."

"You mean *your* money, don't you? You don't give two figs about your son. You want him in jail so you can keep everything he's worked hard for all his life." Thank goodness Florence had some spirit. Unfortunately, I didn't think it was going to help. Unless she managed to prod Catherine into a lunatic rage, although that could go either way. It might help us overcome her, or it might make everything worse.

"It's my money, missy. He made me suffer when he left

me alone, so it's only fair he pays me back, and he wouldn't be where he is today if it wasn't for me."

"What, in jail? You disgust me. Those women you killed weren't after his money. You're the leech, not them." I was so jealous. She was making some great points. I guessed that was why she earned the big bucks.

Catherine smiled and shrugged. "And this is why you're going to be next. I don't take kindly to those who disagree with me. Your attitude is intolerable." Florence's anger melted away with the retreating blood flow from her face. Catherine turned to me. "You get to watch as I take out her deceiving heart and tear her beauty from her skull. She won't tempt anyone after this. And in a few days, it will be your turn." Catherine cackled, fulfilling the witch stereotype with gusto.

I swallowed bile and resisted the urge to flinch. I had to stop this. What the hell could I do? My thoughts raced even faster than my heart. *Think, Lily, think.* There had to be a way. Florence had moved to the back of her cage, as far away from Catherine as she could get. But it wasn't going to be nearly far enough.

Catherine mumbled, and bolts of electricity zapped from bar to bar, from cage ceiling to floor. I didn't feel the warmth I usually felt when it came to the power, but maybe it was because I was trapped in the cage and blocked off from my magic.

"No!" I screamed. "Stop!"

Florence's body flopped around like a fish desperately clinging to life. The sizzle of power stopped, and she collapsed and lay still. My breath sawed in and out, as if I'd just sprinted a hundred-metre race. Was she still alive? *Please, don't be dead.* I leaned forward as far as I could, careful not to touch the bars. Her chest rose and fell ever so slightly. I let out a huge relieved breath and looked up at Catherine. She smiled her evil smile and leaned into the cage.

Catherine gripped Florence's ankles and dragged her out of the cage, her head clunking on the floor as she exited.

Was anyone coming for us? No one knew where I was. And even if I'd told Imani where I'd gone, she wouldn't have found me there. For all I knew, I was in France or Ireland. Catherine could have sent me anywhere when she'd thrown her doorway around me, and she must have set it near the ceiling so I fell out and smashed into the ground. That made sense. My eyes widened. Is that what she'd done to Trudie? Thrown a doorway around Trudie's doorway and sent her here, and in front of all of us? Could someone even do that?

"Ow! Goddammit!" There was a thud. Catherine stood in front of the stainless-steel table after having dropped Florence. I crinkled my face in sympathy... with Florence, not Catherine. She bent but stopped abruptly halfway, slamming her hand onto her back and moaning. Well, well, well, somewitch had a back problem. I smiled.

I rearranged my expression into something I hoped resembled sympathy. "Do you need some help? I can lift her onto the table if you like."

She slowly straightened and turned towards me. Lips pursed, she looked at Florence again, then back up at me.

"Give me a moment to think about it." Catherine took a deep breath and tried bending again. She'd hardly bent when she cried, "Hellfire and damnation! Bloody back."

"I won't try anything. I promise. Maybe if I help you, you can put in a good word for me with Jeremy. He'll need someone to visit him when he's in jail, and he's so handsome. I really do like him, not just his fame and money. Maybe I could take an oath to not tell anyone anything about you and what you've done? If he stays in jail, and you keep his money, and I have my life, we all win." I smiled and nodded, trying to believe my own crap so it would seem legit.

Florence groaned. Nice timing. Catherine walked haltingly towards my cage. Would I have time to cast a return-to-sender spell while shoving her? Or should I wait for a better opportunity? I had no idea how strong her magic was, and I would only get one chance. She reached the cage and mumbled. I tensed and held my breath, just in case she'd been lying to me and rather than let me out, she was going to fry me. The door clicked and swung open.

"Hold your hands out."

I did as asked. Ghostly golden rope appeared in the air, then snaked around my wrists, binding them. A flash of light and moment of searing heat around my wrists and the rope became solid. "Now you may exit."

I stepped out of the cage, emptiness hitting me in the gut. Damn. Looked like I would have to wait for a better time. I could still feel my magic in the cage—it was as if we were separated by a thin invisible barrier—but now that she'd cut me off, all I could sense was emptiness. It was just like wearing PIB handcuffs. Oh joy. I hastily turned my thoughts to birds and double-chocolate muffins. Now my power was gone, she'd be able to read my mind if she possessed that talent. Maybe I should sing a song to myself. What would suit this occasion? Thirty Seconds to Mars for a battle anthem, or maybe Zara Larsen with "Ruin My Life." Hmm, that sounded about right. I laughed.

Catherine tilted her head to the side and smirked. "Maybe you're more like me than I thought. It's good that you find this amusing. You should really enjoy what happens next. Now, pick her up and place her on the table face up."

I planted happy thoughts in my brain, which was trying to reject them, but I was persistent. *Minions, kittens, and chocolate. Minions, kittens, and chocolate.* Hmm, this was going to be harder than I thought. How was I going to pick her up? She probably weighed more than me. As I contemplated the best way to get her onto the table, I glanced around at the various tools and crap scattered about. There were rubber gloves, a scalpel, forceps, a bloody rag.

"Well, I haven't got all day. Hurry up, or I'll put you back in the cage, and you can have your turn on the table tomorrow."

I swallowed hard. Not happening. *Minions, kittens, chocolate.* "Sorry. Just figuring out the best way. It's going to be kind of hard with my wrists tied together."

Catherine huffed and rolled her eyes. "Fine." She mumbled something, and the rope elongated in the middle to the point where I could spread my arms about a metre wide, but I still had no magic access. Damn. "Now stop piddling around. I need a new heart for my collection." She grinned and clapped her hands together excitedly.

I blinked and tried to keep my thoughts neutral, but it was a losing battle. How much longer I could contain my disgust was anyone's guess. Damn everyone at the stupid PIB. If they hadn't been so against me helping Jeremy, maybe I would have told someone what was happening. Maybe I wouldn't be here. *Stop thinking!* Negativity wouldn't help me now. Neither would blaming anyone. It was my own stupid fault for not being careful.

Time to do this and hope an opportunity presented itself. I knelt behind Florence's head and wriggled my hands under her back until I could slide my arms all the way under hers. Once I had them secured near her shoulders, I carefully lifted one knee till I had my foot on the floor, then I lifted the other. While I heaved her up, Catherine slid the rubber gloves on. I couldn't let this happen, and the seconds were ticking down.

Catherine grabbed the scalpel and held it to my chest, just over my heart. "You'd better not be stalling, photo girl. Would you like to go first, after all?"

"What about me helping you? Aren't you going to let me live?"

"I never agreed to that." She laughed. "You must think I'm stupid."

My voice came out strained—Florence was not a feather. "No, of course not. But I thought you'd be a woman with honour." Maybe I could appeal to her sense of pride?

"I'm helping you. I should get something worthwhile in return?"

"I don't think so. When you're done, you can go back in the cage." She wasn't very good at negotiating. Since I'd get nothing out of this, I had nothing to lose. Very bad decision on her part.

My shoulders ached from holding onto Florence for so long, and if I didn't hurry, I was going to drop her. I walked backwards quickly, dragging her with me.

"What do you think you're doing?"

"She's coming back to my cage with me. If you won't deal, I'm not putting her on the table." So there.

"Stop!"

I kept walking.

Her face reddened. "I said stop! Damn you!"

"Why don't you stop me?" Somewhere deep in my brain came the suggestion that maybe I shouldn't be goading her.

She mumbled something, and I hit a barrier. She said something I couldn't decipher, and a large kitchen knife appeared in her hand. Damn. I'd just made it worse. I lowered Florence to the floor and let go of her, then faced Catherine the Crazy. Even though she was walking with a stiff gait, she'd almost reached me. It wasn't like this place was huge.

"Because of your insubordinate attitude, you're going first. I can gut you. It's not ideal, but as long as I can cut your heart out in one piece, I'll be happy."

I tried to back up, but the invisible wall stopped me. Crap. I crabbed sideways, feeling for a break in the barrier.

Reaching the far wall brought me no escape. Catherine hobbled after me. I was backed into a corner. She held the knife out in front of her, but she was slow. I ran towards her, then dodged to the left and kept going. If I couldn't win with witch skills, I'd have to try and outrun her and her magic, which wasn't the best plan, but it was the only one I had.

I reached the metal table and frantically searched for any kind of weapon. Nothing. Was the universe kidding me right now? I jerked my head up at the shuffle, click, shuffle, click of Catherine bearing down on me. She was three metres away—I had plenty of time to run again even though she'd picked up speed. I gauged how much time I'd have to run to the door and escape, but I couldn't leave Florence. She could easily kill her while I was gone, but then again, if I didn't escape, she'd kill both of us. The only solution I could live with was to stop her.

She laughed. "You'll never escape, silly girl. Your feet are stuck to the floor."

What? I tried to lift one foot, then the other. I strained until my muscles burnt. Nothing happened. This being-cut-off-from-magic thing was horrible—I couldn't tell when she was casting a spell. I obviously hadn't tried hard enough. I wasn't going to die like this, with things unsaid to the people I loved, who may have been angry with me, but I knew they still loved me. And there was no way I was leaving this earth without my precious niece or nephew not knowing an aunt's undying love. Damned if I was going to die before he or she was born.

There had to be a way to access the river of magic. Hope flared when I realised I had my innate magic, the power that every witch had in small amounts—their life force. I delved deep inside while watching Catherine inch closer and closer, blade ready to strike. But there was nothing to see. The rope binding my wrists was like a road-block or dam, cutting off my power. Hmm, those things could be broken, given enough force. I concentrated, pushing my lifeforce energy towards the ropes, visualising them separating and dropping to the floor, dissolving. Tingling warmth radiated through my stomach, my headache intensified, and sweat sprang out on my forehead. I winced but asked my body for more. Whatever I had must be given. It was all or I would be nothing. There was no choice.

Florence's pained cry rang out. "Lily, watch out!"

I appreciated the warning, but it was unnecessary. I was all too aware of Catherine pulling her arm back, ready to plunge the knife into my stomach. I sent more of my life-force against the bonds. The sound of wind rushing through trees vibrated my ears, and the warmth in my gut grew to a blazing, blood-boiling inferno. I gritted my teeth, but the pain was too much. I screamed and grabbed my middle, fighting the violent urge to double over.

Catherine's cackle seemed as if it was echoing through a tunnel, distant, muted as her arm started forward. I panted, the pressure building inside me asking for everything and leaving no room for my lungs to expand.

She lunged. The blade, lifeless grey in the faded light,

sliced into me, just below the protection of my arms as I gave one last push, sending everything into the golden rope. My final scream, a razorblade of sound, shredded my throat.

The shackles exploded with a deafening boom that shook the walls and sent a shockwave outward. Ears ringing, I fell back, slamming into the table. The last thing I saw before I crashed into the ground was Catherine's shocked face, replete with capital *O* as she was blasted off her feet and hurtled through the air.

Muffled shouts came from behind the door. Banging, then the sound of wood splintering. So many voices shouting beyond the ringing, "Lily! Lily!" Was one of them James?

I tried to answer, to call out I was here, but I was so very tired, and my mouth wouldn't move. The grating rattle of a hard-won breath filled my ears.

Oh. Was that me?

Dizziness.

I tried but failed to suck in another breath. My eyes closed, and as I bid my loved ones goodbye in my head, my last tear slid down my cold cheek. The golden river beckoned, no longer out of reach beyond the magic shackles, but this time, it ran through a meadow lit with flowers of every colour and dewy grass that sparkled in the morning sun. I reached for the warmth, held it to me for comfort as the shouts and ringing faded to silence.

So this was how it ended.

Crap.

CHAPTER 16

Heavy. So heavy it felt as if my limbs could sink through the bed. I was awake but exhausted. *Maybe I should just turn over and go back to sleep. Hang on a minute....*

My eyes sprang open. My room! I was alive! At least I thought I was.

"You're awake!" Joy radiated from Olivia's face. "Hang on a sec." She jumped off a chair next to my bed and ran to the doorway to yell, "She's awake! Lily's awake!"

Yep, I was alive. But, man, was I sore. Everything ached, and my stomach throbbed. I tried to speak, but my throat and mouth were parched. I coughed instead, then grunted at the pain that sliced through my belly.

Olivia hurried back over and leant down, squishing me in a huge hug. She sniffled against my hair. "Welcome back, gorgeous girl. I missed you." She pulled away and smiled down at me through her tears. Her voice broke as she said, "Don't ever do that again. Ever."

I swallowed and tried to work moisture into my mouth. "I'll try not to." My voice was hoarse, but at least it worked this time. "Can I have some water, please?"

"I'll grab some. Wait here." She turned and laughed, then spun back. "Okay, so you're not likely to go anywhere, but you know."

As soon as she was out the door, James, Beren, Angelica, and Imani rushed in, pushing each other out of the way to get in as quickly as possible. Happiness surged through my exhaustion—by the relieved looks on their faces, they weren't here to yell at me for something. But then the rush of pleasantness disappeared, leaving me deflated. "Where's Will?"

Angelica and James shared a *look*. Sympathy permeated the room, or was it pity? "Don't hold back. Just tell me." My heart was beating way too fast for someone lying in bed doing nothing.

Angelica's gentle smile was worse than her poker face. This was going to be really bad. She waved her hand, indicating she'd made a bubble of silence. "His assignment is going very well, actually, but he's had to go deep undercover, dear. Not even I can talk to him."

"How deep are we talking?" My throat itched. Where was that water?

James sat on the edge of my bed and brushed my hair off my forehead. "He's close to having those agents trust him. We're hoping they'll bring him into the fold. With a bit of luck, he'll make contact with Dana soon. I'm sorry, Lily. I'm sure he'd be here if he could."

"Oh, okay." I stared at the ceiling, blinking my tears away. Was the universe conspiring to keep us apart? Maybe we were never meant to be together. Deep down, I knew I was being a big baby and feeling sorry for myself, but I was too tired to control my emotions.

"Let's not think about Will right now, dear. It will all work out how it's meant to in the end. He's sacrificing a lot to help us find out what happened to your parents. Keep that in mind, okay?" Angelica made a valid point... as usual.

"I know you're right. Sorry. So, is someone going to tell me how I got here? I thought I was never going to see any of you again."

James smiled. "Imani called me when your phone dropped out."

"I never ignore my talent, Lily. I knew you were in danger." Her dark eyes were serious, the tightness at their corners giving her away.

"After she called me, I came here and found your camera on the dining-room table. I scrolled through it and realised you'd been visiting the crime scenes. When I saw the number plate, I looked it up and found it had belonged to Jeremy's mother—she sold the car shortly after her third murder. We went to her house, but she wasn't there. We searched the place and couldn't find any secret rooms."

"So how did you find me? And where the hell was I?"

Angelica said, "You can thank Jeremy for that. Imani went to see him, and he told her about his mother's holiday house down in Brighton. She'd soundproofed a large brick shed in her backyard. We got there just in time, or maybe a little bit late, to be honest." She blushed. I guessed not living up to her own high standards was bound to get to her.

"But you did. I'm still here." I smiled.

"You can thank my nephew for that."

Beren grinned and pushed through everyone to give me a massive cuddle. I said, "Thank you, B. That's twice now you've saved my life."

"Well, you saved mine once, so I'm only one up, and it's not a competition, you know." He laughed.

"We'll see." I grinned. Of course I didn't want anyone to almost die again, but the way life had been lately, it was bound to happen.

Olivia returned with my water. I gingerly sat up, then gulped it down. Water. Sweet, sweet water. "Thanks, Liv."

"My pleasure. And sorry I didn't get back to you with those number-plate details. I was swamped at work, and I didn't realise my phone battery had died. Can you forgive me?"

"There's nothing to forgive." I grabbed her hand and squeezed. "There is something I want to ask. How did Catherine get around her alibi? She must have snuck away from her trip at some point."

James said, "The woman sharing her room wasn't a witch. She tampered with her memories so that when the police questioned her, she swore blind that Catherine had been with her the whole time."

She was a strong witch. I really had been lucky to get

out alive. If it hadn't been for her bad back.... There was one more question I had to ask. "So, is Jeremy out of jail now? He's obviously innocent." I wasn't one to be petty, but I couldn't help my I-told-you-so expression.

Angelica raised a brow. "Yes, Lily, you were right. I'm sorry I didn't support you in your search for answers. We can talk about that later, but for now, someone's been waiting to see you." A knowing smile crossed her face. "He's been here pretty much the whole time you've been asleep, waiting for you to wake up. Three days, to be exact."

My eyes widened. "What? Why?"

James shrugged. "Because he wants to thank you for saving his life, for believing him when no one else would." James looked up at Angelica, regret shining from his eyes. He looked back at me. "Sorry we had a go at you, Lily. You were doing the right thing, and we're sorry."

"Very sorry," Angelica added.

"I'm just glad you don't all hate me."

"Lily!" Liv admonished. "We could never hate you. Never in a million years. You're our Lily, our impossibly silly, stubborn, coffee-swilling Aussie witch. And we wouldn't have you any other way."

I couldn't help but grin. But then I remembered something. "What about Florence? Is she okay?"

Beren smiled. "She was battered and bruised, but James healed her. I had nothing left after working on you. I slept for two days. Oh, and we managed to save Catherine. She almost died in the power surge, but we saved her. She's in jail, charged with murdering twelve women and the attempted murder of two, plus assault, kidnapping, false imprisonment, plus a couple of other minor charges. She'll go to jail for the rest of her undeserved life."

"Well, that's good. I hope she suffers. Crazy cow." Anger constricted my heart. She'd ruined so many lives, including her son's. How did you ever get past the fact that your mother hates you and tried to put you in jail forever?

"Um, Lily, we have one more question." James took my hand and held it. "How did you cause that explosion of power. It was something we've never seen before. And from what Florence said, you were manacled, cut off from your magic. When we found you, you were bleeding out, but worse, your power centre was burnt out. The only thing keeping you alive was your link to the river of magic. Somehow, even unconscious, you managed to stay linked. If it wasn't for that...."

Five sets of eyes peered at me expectantly. I stared at the bedspread, admiring the scatter of blue fairy wrens on it as I sifted through my brain for the answer. That part was still fuzzy—maybe I'd damaged my brain in the "power explosion." I took a deep breath and looked at everyone in turn as I spoke. "I was manacled with a golden rope made of magic—Catherine's magic. She was going to stab me... she did stab me." Fear shot adrenaline through me, and I was suddenly very awake. I swallowed. "I... I didn't want to die. I didn't want her to kill Florence either. I drew on my life-force and pushed it towards the blockage of power, the rope. Eventually I drew enough that it exploded. But I realised I'd drawn too much. I knew I was dying. But when I broke the bonds, the golden river and a meadow appeared. I settled into the warmth, drew it into me. It was like going to sleep wrapped in cosy blankets. I'd said goodbye to all of you in my mind." When I finished, I wasn't the only one with tears in their eyes, and James might have even been a little awed. I guessed what I'd done was another first and supposed to be impossible. Impossible, as I was learning, was just a word.

Rather than tears, Angelica stared at me with a blank expression. Processing? I guessed even the most experienced of us was sometimes shocked. I smiled at her and shrugged. She returned my smile. "We'll talk about this later, Lily."

"I know." My smile widened to a grin—it was awesome to have a *later*.

"Um, did you all forget?" asked Imani.

"Ooh, yes. You can tell her," said Angelica.

"From now on, I'm your personal bodyguard. Whenever you're on PIB business, or doing things behind their backs"—she gave me a we-all-know-it's-bound-to-happen-again look—"I'm going with you. I promise to keep your secrets, but you're not allowed to do anything remotely dangerous without me at your side. Understood?" She folded her arms, her gaze stern and inviting no argument, which was fine—I didn't have the energy to argue today.

"Okay."

"Just like that, *okay*? No tricks?" She seemed confused.

"Ha ha, no tricks. I trust you, Imani, and after what just happened, I'd be an even bigger idiot than usual to refuse. Thanks for offering." Who was this Lily, and what had they done with the real me?

"Good then." She nodded, a small smile curving her lips.

"Can I interrupt?" Liv asked.

"Yes, dear."

"Jeremy's desperate to say thank you to our star witch. I think we should give them some privacy."

"Um, maybe I should get dressed." I didn't want to be in my pyjamas in front of him, and with no bra. Hell, no. "Everyone out. I'm not ready to use my magic again. My tummy's sore and I'm exhausted."

Beren nodded. "Good idea. The soreness isn't just because of the knife wound, which I healed, by the way. Your magic centre will be weak for a few more days, so go easy on the magic."

"Consider it done. Now, out."

When everyone had left, and the door was shut, I slowly dressed, grunting with the effort and pain as I went. When I'd finished, I sat back on my bed, and there was a knock on the door. "Come in."

Jeremy entered, his blue eyes bright yet warm, the darkness under them gone. He grinned, movie-star looks back in place. There was still an undercurrent of sadness about him though. "Mind if I come in?"

"Of course not. It's not every day a girl has a movie star in her bedroom." I waggled my eyebrows.

"It's not every day I'm in the bedroom of the bravest woman in the world."

"I wouldn't quite say that. I'd say one-part brave, two-parts stupid." I laughed, then groaned and pressed my palm against my stomach. Jeremy's brows drew together. "It's okay, Jay. I'm fine. Just a bit of residual pain. I'll have to stop laughing at my own jokes for a while. It's going to be tough."

He laughed and shook his head. "You're one in a bazillion, Lily. I just wanted to say thank you a thousand times over for getting me out of there. I'm also so very sorry my mother tried to kill you. I'm still trying to come to terms with what she's done." He set his jaw, anger flaring from his gaze. He sat on the chair next to my bed. "Do you mind?" He reached over and took my hand in his soft, warm one.

I ignored the delicate flutter of unwanted butterflies. Will would find his way back to me. I knew he would. "I'm sorry it was your mum too. You deserve better than a parent like that."

"It is what it is. She's sick, but still, I never want to speak to her again. I feel like vomiting when I think about what she's done. Anyway, I don't want to talk about it anymore. My counsellor can help me find my way through the bomb-sites that are my heart and brain right now. I'd rather spend this time telling you how special you are. You believed in me when no one else did. You saw me—not the famous guy on the big screen, but the young boy who only ever wanted his mother's love. I could never reach her, Lily…." His eyes glistened. I squeezed his hand. "Anyway"—he swallowed—"I didn't come here to make you cry. You need to know that I care about you. No one has ever done anything like this for me. You risked your life, and for that, I will be forever grateful. Anything you want, just ask. I'd like us to be friends, Lily. Is that okay?"

My smile was wide. "That's more than okay, Jay. Whenever you need to talk, I'm here. You're a good guy, and I can never have too many good people in my life." I bit my lip, remembering what Liv had asked. "So... there is something I want." His eyebrows rose in question. "Can I get your autograph?"

He burst into laughter, his eyes wrinkling at the corners. "I thought you weren't a fan?"

"I promised Liv, actually."

"Yeah, sure you did." He laughed some more.

I swatted his arm. "Just hand it over, movie guy."

"Anything for you, Lily. You're the real star in this room."

I rolled my eyes. That was a big call, one I didn't agree with, and seeing as how Liv had said the same thing, I had some huge expectations to live up to. Funnily enough, it didn't bother me. I'd do it all again if I had to. Injustice had no place in my world.

Nevertheless, I did send a little request to the universe not to send anything my way for a while. I deserved a break, dammit. Christmas was coming, and it would be the first one I'd be spending with family in six years. It would be super wonderful to be able to relax and enjoy it.

Jeremy handed me two signed photos. "One for you, and one for Liv."

"Did you just magic those here?"

"Yes, why?"

I tensed my forehead. "I didn't feel it… your magic." What if I never got it back? Vertigo hit, and I swallowed the urge to vomit.

Jeremy's eyes widened. "Are you all right? You're rather pale." I shook my head. I couldn't say the words in case it made my worst fear come true. "It'll be okay, Lily. James said you burnt yourself out fighting my mother. I'm sure you'll be back to normal in no time. The important thing is that you're alive. Everything else will fall into place later. I promise." He grabbed my hand and squeezed. "I have to go now. My agent has lined up a year's worth of interviews. Real life beckons." The poor guy. He'd have to talk about how horrible his mother was. That would have to hurt.

"Good luck."

"Thanks." He bent and embraced me. "Don't be a stranger."

"I can't promise I won't get stranger."

He squished me harder as he vibrated with laughter. Then he let go and stood straight. "Until next time." He flashed me a grin and stepped through his doorway. The room was much emptier without him, but he had his life to live, and I had mine. At least we both had *lives* now.

I looked down at his headshots. He'd signed one, *To Liv, look after Lily. Jeremy xx*. But mine, oh, um. *To the most amazing woman I know. You're a hard act to follow. If you ever need a leading man, give me a call. I'd love to be part of your happy ending. Yours cornily, Jay. xx*

I blushed, and there was no stopping my goofy grin.

Damn him for being so sweet and funny and corny. But right now, my heart belonged to Will.

"Hey, Lily. Has Jeremy gone?" Liv stood in the doorway.

"Yes, and he left a little something for you." She came in and sat in the chair. It was sure seeing a lot of action today. I handed her the picture.

She squeed and danced in her chair. "Well, it's about time! I thought you'd forgotten."

"Me forget? Never." I winked.

"I should have known you'd come through. You always do."

"It's my job as your best friend. Didn't you know?"

Olivia grinned. "And it's my job as your best friend to keep you in coffees and double-chocolate muffins. I'm going to duck up to Costa and grab you some. You haven't eaten for three days."

My stomach rumbled like a B-double truck speeding over potholes. "Splendid idea. I'll be waiting eagerly. Hopefully my stomach won't have eaten itself by then."

She waved and left me with my thoughts. There were so many—good, bad, scary, sweet, and painful—it would likely take my entire recuperation to make sense of them. I took a deep breath, steeled my heart, and started sifting.

ACKNOWLEDGMENTS

As usual, Becky, Chryse, and Mandy have picked up my slops and fixed the mistakes. Thank you, ladies! Hubby and kids have also been patient while I wrote my little heart out, so thanks, guys. And to the readers who are always there, waiting for the next book—I can't thank you enough. We make a great team.

ABOUT THE AUTHOR

USA Today bestselling author, Dionne Lister is a Sydneysider with a degree in creative writing, two Siamese cats, and is a member of the Science Fiction and Fantasy Writers of America. Daydreaming has always been her passion, so writing was a natural progression from staring out the window in primary school, and being an author was a dream she held since childhood.

Unfortunately, writing was only a hobby while Dionne worked as a property valuer in Sydney, until her mid-thirties when she returned to study and completed her creative writing degree. Since then, she has indulged her passion for writing while raising two children with her husband. Her books have attracted praise from Apple iBooks and have reached #1 on Amazon and iBooks charts worldwide, frequently occupying top 100 lists in fantasy. She's excited to add cozy mystery to the list of genres she writes. Magic and danger are always a heady combination.

ALSO BY DIONNE LISTER

Printed in Great Britain
by Amazon

41865963R00144